Also Available From Jacy Morris

Fiction:

1000 Pieces of Sweet (Coming Soon)
The Abbey
The Drop
Killing the Cult
The Lady That Stayed
The Pied Piper of Hamelin
The Taxidermied Man
An Unorthodox Cure

One Night Stand at the End of the World Series
One Night Stand at the End of the World
One Night Stand in the Wastes
One Night Stand in Ike

The Enemies of Our Ancestors Series
The Enemies of Our Ancestors
The Cult of the Skull
Broken Spirits

This Rotten World Series
This Rotten World
This Rotten World: Let It Burn
This Rotten World: No More Heroes
This Rotten World: Winter of Blood
This Rotten World: Choking on the Ashes
This Rotten World: Rally and Rot

One Night Stand in the Wastes

By Jacy Morris

Table of Contents

Chapter 1: Deathstyles of the Poor and the Unknown

The land to the east of Shithole descended into the burnt mist of the wastes, sloping downward imperceptibly like a bathtub leading to a drain. In that drain, accumulated hair, boogers, ejaculations, nothing you wanted to look too closely at. To the uninitiated, the flowery fields to the east of Shithole might seem like a walk in the park. Of course, the comedian knew better.

He knew the world had turned upon itself, rising up against humans so everything that had once been taken for granted had to be questioned—even this flowery field. Despite the fuzzy squirrels bounding among the dandelions and buttercups and the bees flitting from flower to flower collecting pollen, the comedian knew there was a darkness there. For every benign version of a thing, there was a malignant version, ready to take a man's life.

Is this a regular sunflower, or the type that likes to spray acid in a person's face? Is this your regular old honeybee, or the type of bee that likes to sting you to death with a hundred of its friends and then make a nest out of your rotting corpse for their queen? Is that a regular old squirrel, or the type of squirrel that will leap at a man's jugular and rip his neck open with their two front teeth?

A regular old dipshit might ask themselves those questions, but not the comedian. For the comedian, he just assumed everything wanted to kill him. It was safer that way, and while it kept him from doing fun stuff like frolicking in a field of grass with the squirrels like the asshole actor in a douche commercial or erectile dysfunction ad, he found he didn't actually miss the frolicking. Cavorting, yes—frolicking, no.

For this reason, the comedian strode through the field, swerving around the head-height flowers as a matter of principle. They still spit their poison at him, but he walked away unscathed.

When a squirrel stopped its nut collecting and bared its teeth at him, all he did was shoot it the finger and say, "Beat it, ya bucktoothed nutbag." The creature scurried off, probably to find twenty or thirty of its friends to come back and swarm his ass. Not looking forward to a squirrel squareoff, he picked up the pace. It seemed like every deadly thing in the world had thirty friends waiting around a corner—well, everything except for him.

As a bee buzzed in his direction, he whipped out his hand, his thumb and forefinger forming a circle. He snapped his forefinger in mid-air and the bee, concussed by the force of the comedian's flicking finger, flew through the air and landed on its back, its tiny insect legs kicking at the air. Soon, it would right itself and rally a mob of its stinging buddies to deliver vengeance. By the time that happened, the comedian would be long gone. He picked up his pace again, his hips complaining as his stride lengthened.

Near the edge of the thicket of flowers, with the orange light above pounding off his skin, he stumbled on something. Screaming and flailing, he reached for his feet to make sure no hidden vines were getting ready to wrap around his ankles and drag him to the underworld.

It's just a skull, Oddrey said.

As thoughts of his own death evaporated into thin air, he sat up, Oddrey dangling from his jacket pocket.

"You're right." He plucked up the skull and turned it in his hand. For a moment, he held it up to his eyes, about to perform some Shakespearian-type shit, and then something in the back of his head told him the skull was too small, that he shouldn't be touching it. At this, he threw the skull into the grass, laying a trap for the next ignorant person who traipsed through the flowery field of death.

Getting to his feet, he heard three dozen tiny paws rushing through the tall grass.

"That's our cue!" he yelled, and together, Oddrey and the comedian fled the field. His equipment weighed him down, preventing him from running as fast as he wanted. Behind him, the insane chittering of territorial squirrels hit him like a whip, driving him faster. Thirty squirrels would be tough to defeat. They were too small, too many of them. By the time he beat them off, they would have nibbled him to death. No, it was better to run than to beat off squirrels.

As he sprinted through the flowery field, he made a mental note of that advice. If he ever settled down and wrote his book about the wasteland, he thought his advice about squirrels would make a good chapter title.

Eventually, the squirrels, not known for long periods of focused activity, faded away, their squeaks and screams only barely audible. Breathing a sigh of relief, the comedian slowed. The wastes were large, seemed to grow larger every year. It would be wise to conserve any energy he could.

You were scared, Oddrey said.

"Pssh! You're scared. You're the one with no arms or legs. I could take a hundred squirrels."

You didn't say you weren't scared.

"Just because someone doesn't say they're not scared doesn't mean they are scared. That's basic math, basic physics, if you know what I mean."

You don't even know what you mean.

The comedian fell silent at this, mostly because it was true. You couldn't win an argument with Oddrey; it wasn't possible. She seemed to know everything he knew, and even when he lied to her, she had a way of sniffing it out. A thought crossed his mind for a moment, a wild, crazy thought. The clouds in his mind began to part, but then a wild screech from the blasted orange clouds above drove him to the ground. A patch of squirmy grass tickled his cheek as he scanned the sky above, searching for the source of the shriek, for surely it had come from above.

"Did you hear that, Odd? Death from above! You better keep quiet." Slowly, the comedian crawled through the grass, hoping the creature that circled the clouded skies didn't notice him. If it did, it would mean a fight, and he didn't have the time for a tussle. With every second he wasted, Cheatums put more distance between them. This would not stand.

As he turned, craned his neck, and rolled over on his hip, he spied it in the sky, a small black dot circling the flowery field. Batting away a strand of curious grass, he watched as the shape let loose another of those ear-piercing shrieks. The creature's call was not just high-pitched, but painfully so. He was lucky it flew high in the sky. If it blasted that shriek within thirty feet of the comedian, he might lose his hearing. All senses were vital, but especially hearing, for when the sun went down, sound might be the only warning of an approaching danger in the wastes.

That's where he was headed now—the wastes. The people around Shithole thought they had it bad, but their little town was a paradise compared to the actual wastes, that crappy part of the country between the west coast and the east coast. There, anything could happen. Putting up your ridiculous town sign made of spoons and old toothbrushes wasn't even done in most of the clapboard, last-stand cities in the wastes. Everyone in those places knew they were living on borrowed time. It was hard to pretend you weren't when the entirety of your environment seemed to want you dead. On the coasts, you could fool yourself. In the middle of the country, on the other side of the mountains, that was impossible.

Eventually, the shrieker dove from the sky, plummeting to the ground a mere thirty feet behind him. Even with his hands over his ears, he could hear the soul-penetrating scream of the abomination. It landed with a thump, scooping up rabid squirrels by the armful. With a crack of its wings, it launched itself into the sky, sending dandelion seeds fluttering through the air. Each seed floated like a miniature, rootless tree. When he was young, he had called them wishes. Now he knew they were just another part of the world that wanted man dead. How could they not? Man had been calling dandelions weeds for so long that humans seemed to have forgotten the beauty of the small white umbrellas as they twirled through the air like fairies in a ballet.

When the shrieker disappeared into the clouds, the comedian pushed himself to his feet, dusting himself off with his fingerless gloves. A dandelion seed, a wish, floated through the air, swirling past his nose like a curious bug, and he held out his hand. It landed on his palm, he closed his eyes and prepared to make a—

I wish for a body.

"Not cool, Odd. That was my wish," he whispered, but he blew on the small seedling anyway since Oddrey couldn't do it herself. It rode his breath, twirling through the air, spinning for a moment before the comedian turned away. *It was best not to see where one's wish landed.*

As he took a step forward, a skinless squirrel corpse fell from the sky and landed with a soft crash, sending up another puff of dandelion wishes. Somewhere in the orange clouds, the shrieker was enjoying its feast, tossing squirrel bodies to the ground like a lazy farmer finished with a half-eaten apple core.

He pointed at the skinless squirrel and said, "Look! Your wish came true! There's your body, Odd."

Haha.

11

With a smile on his face, the comedian trudged onward, plunging into the waste fog clinging to the edge of the grassy field.

****

Each step he took drove the waste fog back, as if a force field existed around him, a bubble of normality the fog couldn't dare hope to penetrate. The fog made being cautious almost useless. You never knew what would pop out of the fog. All around him, the air reeked of burnt flesh. The wind was not strong today, and the ashes of the world puffed into the air with each footstep.

On and on he walked, practicing his jokes, sharpening his mind on the whetstone of his own knowledge. It was a cannibalistic exercise. He lived in a world where no knowledge was new, but for the knowledge of how to survive the horrors of the wastes, and gaining that knowledge could get one killed or skinned and dropped from a thousand feet. *Fucking shriekers.*

"I'll give you something to shriek about, ya whiny little fuck." He said this low, almost in a whisper. Superstition, once frowned upon, had become a survival skill all its own in the wasteland. No one could explain how one person survived and another one didn't. Even now, that gang of rabid squirrels was probably huddled around their dead friend, making up little rules about why they had survived and Nibbles and Scratchy Ass hadn't. The comedian was not a superstitious man for the most part, but he was prudent.

You swear too much, Oddrey said.

"What the fuck are you blathering about?"

You swear too much. You think it's clever, but it's not.

"What do you know about it? You're a goddamn doll head."

12

I know that you're lazy, and sometimes you rely on swearing to cover up for the fact that you're not all that funny.

"I don't see you doing stand-up. If you know so much, why don't you do a set in the next town we're in."

I'm shy.

"Everyone's a fucking critic… sorry. Everyone is a fudging critic."

See? It's funnier already.

Out of the fog, a structure appeared, nothing amazing like the Gates of Heaven or the Gates of Hell, but a random building, two-floors high. Busted windows greeted him, their broken glass coated in a layer of dust that made the jagged shards still jutting from the frames resemble a raider's filthy teeth.

"You ever heard of Robin Leach, Odd?"

I've heard of robins. I've heard of leeches, but I have yet to see a combination of the two.

In his best impression of a British, bourgeois television host, the comedian announced, "Well today, my empty-headed friend, you're on Lifestyles of the Poor and the Unknown."

What are you doing?

"A bit."

I have a feeling this is going to be longer than a bit.

"Righty-o, my posh, socialite chum."

The comedian stopped and froze, testing his sixth sense to see if it tingled at all. While he wasn't a hundred-percent sure his sixth sense was real, it had saved him enough times to be more than just superstition—maybe—probably. Nothing tickled on the back of his neck, so he continued around to the front of the building. A small sign sat half buried in gray-green ash, but he could just make out the name of the building. It was supposed to read *West Slope Apartments*, but the E in the word Slope had been burned off.

13

"Welcome to the West Slop Apartments, a posh getaway for those of medium means. Formerly known as the West Slope Apartments, the name was changed when the original owners were burned alive in a nuclear holocaust. Now under new management, by no one, the West Slop is home to all sorts of creepy crawlies, and perhaps even a skeleton or two."

I hate that accent.

The comedian stepped forward, his boots grinding grime into the concrete stoop that stuck out like a tongue from the front of the building. Despite its run-of-the-mill nature, the comedian wondered how the building had gotten there. The ground all around it was unpaved, populated with tumbleweeds and various other plants of non-importance. But that was the wastes for you. One minute you were walking in a burnt fog of charred existence, and the next, you would stumble upon an almost completely intact structure that appeared out of nowhere. Sometimes it was a gift, sometimes it was a curse. You could never tell what you'd get. It was best not to think about it.

Then he thought about it. In his mind, he pictured the apartment complex flying through the air in a wicked, massive dustnado, spinning and twirling like Dorothy's house in Oz. It was the only explanation for why a building like this could just appear out of nowhere with nothing around it. That or he had been transported to someone's twisted version of a massive Monopoly board, and this was the shitty hotel someone had plopped down. "It's definitely a Mediterranean Avenue."

When he pulled on the door's handle, the entire door fell out of the frame. He grasped the door by its edges, waddled it to the side, and leaned it against the wall of the apartment complex.

"A bit of a fixer-upper, I guess." Kicking up undisturbed dust, he stepped into the gloom of the building.

14

"Here you find the grand entrance, complete with pathetic skeletons curled up in a ball. Did they die of nuclear radiation, starvation, or too much caviar? We may never know."

It's getting old.

"Everything gets old, Odd. That's how time works. It's the way of the world. The sooner you realize that, the sooner you can be a cantankerous old shit like me."

Stepping over the pathetic skeletons on the floor, their arms locked around each other, the comedian turned left. The hallway oozed darkness, and he pressed a convenient switch. The twinkle lights wrapped around his chest like a bandolier sparkled to life, and by their hazy light, he navigated across a hallway filled with rat droppings and dust.

At the first door, he raised a fist and said, "Let's see if anyone's home."

The door rattled in its frame as he pounded on it five times. Each thunderous blow echoed throughout the building. If there was anyone there, they would have heard him, but all he heard was the scurrying of rats in the dark places of the building.

No one's home.

"That's funny. Our production manager assured me he'd confirmed with the owner."

You're not on a show.

"Life's a show, Odd." The comedian patted himself down. "Now, let's see where I left that key. That's the secret to being a good production manager. Always be prepared for any eventuality. Ah! Here it is." The comedian reared back and kicked the door open.

Entering through a broken window, a foul, singed wind swirled the dust in the apartment, and crawling things ran for the corners, but nothing greeted the comedian with imminent danger, so he stepped inside. Continuing in his

Robin Leach voice, he said, "Here we have a rather posh domicile—"

You're using the word posh too much.

"—complete with natural air-conditioning. The apartment has all the apocalyptic flair one could ever dream of. Dust on the ground, roaches in the walls, and what's that I smell? The rot of an old corpse! Let's see what's in the kitchen."

The grit of the apartment crunched underneath his boots. Out of habit, the comedian flicked the switch for the lights, but nothing came on. In front of him stood a standard-issue kitchenette, small and unimpressive. The apartment was little more than a box for people to sleep in before they had to drag their ass to work and slave away the day to pay the rent.

The comedian didn't bother with the refrigerator. Anything in there would be long spoiled by now. The cupboard doors swung open silently, and he peered into the darkness of each cupboard. Dishes, plates, glasses, he swept these all to the floor where they landed and crashed apart. *What good was a plate without any food to eat off it?*

As he had predicted, he found nothing. He left the kitchen a mess, so the next person would know not to bother. He was good like that.

In the bedrooms, he found nothing but sad pictures and a rotted body. In a wallet, he found a driver's license for one Marcus Hoiberg. The license had been issued in Illinois. As far as the comedian could tell, they were a long way from Illinois. As he continued his search through the house, he began to wonder at the apartment building's presence. *Was this an Illinois apartment building? If so, how did it get here in the west?*

These questions tumbled around his mind, and then he put them away, placed them in cupboards like dishes that would never be used. He could have found the answers to his questions, could have satisfied them completely, but

16

in the end, it didn't matter. He purposefully ignored the addresses on the envelopes in the apartment's hallway. He imagined God had been playing Monopoly with another god when one of them had bumped the board in a drunken stupor and sent the pieces flying all over the world. He assumed all gods were drunk all the time. Hell, he'd be sloshed all day if he had to listen to all those prayers from the desperate and dying.

In the bathroom, he lifted the lid off the toilet tank, only to find it was bone dry. In the bowl, a ring of ancient toilet scum moldered, dry and brown. Out of the corner of his eye, he caught sight of a cockroach. With a barely imperceptible shake of his head, he let it continue its life, such as it was. *I'm not that desperate—yet.*

The apartment was a bust. Even the clothes in the dresser crumbled to dust as he lifted the shirts out. Exiting, he plodded through the hallway, though he knew he needed to hurry. His energy was low, and the Vienna sausage and old pasta he'd been running on seemed to have worked its way through his system.

The next door opened easily, and all he had to do was take one quick look into the apartment to see it had been tossed already. Based upon the fact that the locked doors still held untouched apartments, he assumed the complex had been looted soon after the bombs dropped, when people still held onto some semblance of their humanity. Ignoring the mess, he stepped into the apartment. *Might still be something good in here, maybe. Probably not.*

He trampled over old books, their paper yellowed, the covers faded. He kicked them to the side as if they were nothing more than tiny skulls in the wild. A book couldn't do anything anymore. The words inside were painful, filled with descriptions of a world that could never be again. No one read anymore. Reading was pain, a reminder of what had been lost.

In the bedrooms, he discovered fragile clothes scattered about, an old vibrator with a corroded battery compartment, pictures so sweet they made his teeth hurt— no, wait, his teeth hurt because he was actually gritting them. With an almost audible creak, he forced his jaw to open, and he flexed the muscles there. He tasted the dust in the air, so thick he wanted to spit it out, but he couldn't afford to waste the moisture.

With a trembling hand, he reached out and placed the picture frames facedown, then he moved onto the bathroom. Floss, waxed and minty. *It's something, I guess.* Underneath the sink, he found rolls of toilet paper that crumbled even as he picked them up. A shame. A pristine roll could feed a man for a week in the right town. People missed having a clean ass.

After tossing the floss in one of his many pockets, he moved onto the closets. Jackets… there were always jackets, but he had no need of a jacket. His officer's jacket was more than enough, and it showed virtually no wear. Constructed of durable materials that seemed to weather the apocalypse just fine, the found jackets were worth a fortune, but he couldn't afford to carry the weight, not with dwindling supplies and an unknown stretch of waste to cross. He checked the spare boots and shoes in the closet. They were small, too small for him, especially the child-sized galoshes.

He closed the closet door behind him, feeling tense. The comedian hated to be inside, didn't trust the walls, didn't trust he would be able to escape. Still, after checking the other trashed apartments, he forced himself up to the second floor. The stairs groaned underneath his weight, and at any moment, he expected them to crack underneath his feet and plunge him into the splintery darkness beneath the staircase.

The second floor was much the same, empty rooms, cleaned-out cupboards, broken crockery, and shattered windows. In one of the rooms, he trapped a thick cockroach with his hand, so it wasn't a complete loss. Protein was protein, though he hated the small piece of exoskeleton that became lodged between his back molars. Sucking on his teeth and trying to dislodge the crunchy morsels from between his teeth with his tongue, he stumbled into another room.

Among faded children's books with gold-foil spines and a wall decorated in garish colors, he found something fantastic, a small, child-sized piano. He squatted down, one arm dangling between his legs as he pressed on one of the white keys. The keys felt like cheap plastic to his fingertips, but the sound singing forth from the miniscule piano was anything but cheap. Rich and somewhat high, he pressed more of the keys and let the reverberation of the small wires inside wash over him. It was badly out of tune, but he could fix that.

The piano reminded him of something one of Charlie Brown's friends would play. It was a child's toy, but it was more than that to the comedian. He picked it up off the ground, weighing it in his hands, trying to decide if the weight was worth it. In the end, he decided he would never see anything like it again, so he hoisted it up on his back, wrapped it in a jacket from a hall closet, and secured it with forgotten leather belts to his backpack.

In the hallway once more, the light had dimmed as the clouds outside had thickened. The twinkle light bandolier faded quickly and then died altogether. Now shrouded in complete darkness and surrounded by walls, an unwanted memory bubbled up, sharp and terrible. The gloom of the apartment building overwhelmed him, and shaking, he stumbled out into the fading orange day, willing to leave the rest of the apartment's treasures untouched for the next traveler who stumbled along. *That's what good guys do.*

19

With a trembling hand, he pulled the dental floss from his pocket, sliced off a length, and placed it in his mouth. The floss's mint coating induced his salivary glands to explode, and he stepped deeper into the wastes, forgetting about the apartment building as soon as the fog behind him closed in upon it.

Further into the wastes, the suffocating darkness all but forgotten, he took the now-flavorless floss from his mouth, straightened it out in his fingers, and then began flossing. His body shook with the energy gained from the faintly sugary coating of the waxed thread. It wouldn't last long, but he enjoyed it while he could.

The ground before him was flat, dusty. Yellowed grasses, long dead, crunched under his boots, and he strode forward, pausing every now and then to scan the orange sky, lest the shrieker appeared out of nowhere to dive down upon him. While staring at the billowing clouds above, he imagined apartment buildings and other structures floating through the air, still circling the earth after its cataclysmic upheaval.

As he watched the clouds storm across the sky, he imagined a house crashing down upon him. "You think my legs would curl up like the Wicked Witch of the East, Odd?"

I don't know what you're talking about.

The comedian finished digging out the filth from between the last of his molars. Now tinged pink by his blood, he tossed the floss upon the ground and swallowed his bloody saliva. If he encountered a trader, he'd have to keep the floss off the table. Gingivitis could kill just as surely as a divebombing shrieker.

On he walked, sucking at his bleeding gums, savoring the tang of salt on his tongue, and resisting the urge to pull a thick wad of floss free from the spool to chew on.

****

As the orange sky dimmed and he stumbled across another location, he got the feeling like maybe he was on the edge of a town. Crumbled asphalt, now nothing more than a field of rocks with dried brush sticking up through the cracks, surrounded another building that seemed out of place. Larger than the apartment building, the place had the functional feel of something industrial. He circled the building at a distance which allowed him to scan the walls of the building through the waste fog.

His lungs burned from breathing the particulates in the air, and he needed to get inside to give his poor lungs a rest. Scouting for signs of a raider presence, he walked around the building. This would make a perfect base for the greedy bastards. After his third circuit, he approached the front doors, confident no one was home. On the glass, he saw the faded remnants of a sign, and he studied it with his head cocked to the side for a moment. Finally, he was able to puzzle out the words of the faded sign. *Midday Cheese Factory.*

It wasn't a company he had ever heard of. He reached out for the door, expecting it to be fully locked, but the heavy glass door swung open with only a slight groan of complaint. Dusting off the atmospheric ash that had accumulated on his jacket throughout the day, he stepped inside.

"Do ya hanker for a hunk of cheese?"
You know I'm lactose intolerant.
"I think you're just plain intolerant."
Haha.

Inside, the comedian explored the ruins, finding copious amounts of faded machinery, dusty metal that could be turned into anything if one knew a smith. Again, it was too much weight to carry.

Sadly, the factory was devoid of cheese. Perhaps an army of rats had come along and carted it all off. Light bled through the factory windows set high in the walls, and he laid out his solar cells to charge his twinkle lights while he examined the tiny piano on the dusty concrete floor.

"Whaddya think?"

I think it's stupid. Can you even play?

"I don't play. I dominate."

He pressed on the keys, soaking up their discordant tunes. He could hear their true tones buried in the slack piano strings.

Sounds like you're choking a cat.

"Yeah, yeah. Just wait." He lifted the lid of the piano and fiddled inside. Each string was fitted with a tiny knob like those on the head of a guitar. As he tapped on the keys he tightened and loosened the strings, ever so slowly, lest he snap one of them. A piano with even one busted string was worthless. Over the course of hours, he tapped and twisted until he managed to shape the miniature piano into some semblance of playability. It wasn't perfect, but it was good enough for now.

He cracked his knuckles, wiggled his fingers like a magician ready to pull off a difficult trick, and played the simplest of tunes, his thick, wasteland fingers transforming into dainty digits of creation. "Twinkle, twinkle little star."

Ugh, Oddrey said.

The comedian sat back, admiring his work, and covered the piano once more. He hoisted it onto his back and left the Midday Cheese Factory. Though he had technically discovered nothing in the factory, he felt richer than when he had entered, and he could breathe right again.

I hope you know better songs than that.

"I'm just getting started."

****

All things being considered, the day had been a pretty good day. Any day where you only experienced a mild form of terror and claustrophobia was a good day. Out in the open, he felt in control, like there wasn't anything he couldn't handle. It was a complete lie, but it was a good one to trick yourself into believing.

Above, the orange sky dimmed, the faint glow of night green replacing the orange pigment. While he could have stayed in the cheese factory, he hadn't gained enough ground. Ike was still several days away, whatever the hell that was.

In his travels, the comedian had seen plenty of towns and settlements. At first, they had all been fairly similar, populated by broken, bashful people who were trying to cope with the total loss of their entire world. As his travels took him across the shattered land, time passed, and with each passing day, the world seemed to grow weirder, stranger, more twisted.

The people in those towns had no clue exactly how bizarre they were, how strange they had become. They were too close to the burning fire of insanity. But the comedian, with the clarity he was known for, could see just how twisted the survivors had grown. Every town was a new adventure, a new budding society with its own rules, mores, and systems. If the world ever calmed down and decided it didn't want to die, then those towns would grow into cities, those cities would become city-states, and the cycle of humanity would begin over again, with every ignorant asshole thinking the place they were born was the greatest in the world, simply because the government told them so.

The folly of nationalism played in his mind for miles until a school bus reared up out of the waste fog. The bus had been old before the end of time, before the day the earth turned. The words *Glenns Ferry School District* were emblazoned on its side. It rested on rusted rims, the rubber

23

tires nothing more than a memory. It looked like a giant block of cheese, and the windows were covered with dust. The rear end of the bus sat canted in the air, the front end resting comfortably in a ditch.

As the green isotopes overhead began their nightly show, the comedian stepped up to the folding door of the bus. He placed his hand on the door and when it didn't open, he grasped the edge and pried it open with a squeal. A skeleton in a school uniform, hidden by the dust on the glass doors, dropped at the comedian's feet. Its small skull rolled free, and the comedian hopped back, reaching for Rib-Tickler, the dagger strapped to his thigh. A foul air wafted from the bus, but it wasn't anything he hadn't smelled before. Though the smell was revolting, it's familiarity comforted him.

He stepped inside the bus, just as he heard the booming howl of a shrieker above. The windows of the bus rattled, and dust drifted down from the frames.

Looks like we're sleeping here, whether we like it or not, Oddrey said.

"Looks like it," he whispered.

Inside the bus, he discovered more skeletons. The largest one sat slumped over the giant steering wheel. On the inside of the cracked windshield, ancient brown stains had dried in a starburst pattern. He kicked out at the corpse, and it leaned back in its chair. Its skin was mummified, and the crushed forehead of the bus driver told him everything he needed to know. After a quick rummage through the man's pockets, he found ancient sticks of gum, dried to a concrete consistency. Other than that, it was a corpse of utter uselessness. He took the bundle of bones and dried skin and threw it out the door of the bus.

Then he prepared himself for the horror inside. It wasn't often he chose to keep his twinkle lights off, but that evening was one of those nights.

The story of the dead played out before him, as if he could see the past in his mind. A school bus, on its way from school, a bus driver with a cracked skull, a pile of small corpses. Something had caused the bus to wreck, and the children, with nowhere to go and with no world to help them, had died. The total lack of candy and food in their backpacks told him the tale. They had starved here, waiting for help, their dead bus driver slowly rotting away. The comedian couldn't tell if they were the lucky ones or not. *Better to die at the beginning than to have to fight to survive.*

Then why do you do it? Oddrey asked.

"You know why."

You don't even know why.

"Shut up, Odd." His words were not unkind; he simply didn't want to think about Oddrey's question. With little ceremony, he dragged the corpses from the bus. Though he should have done it, he couldn't make himself rummage through their tiny pockets. But their backpacks were a different story. Inside, he found all sorts of garbage—assignments, textbooks, long dead cell phones, empty candy wrappers and lunch boxes.

It was a giant pile of nothing. With the bus cleared, he set his possessions on the cracked vinyl seats and lay down for a long night's nap.

Periodically, he would awaken, startled by the call of the shrieker above as it rattled the windows of the bus with its scream.

Sometime in the middle of the night, Oddrey asked, *Did you ride the bus to school?*

"I did."

What was it like?

He couldn't fault Odd for wanting to know. Much of the world was a mystery to her. "It was something. The screaming, the yelling. Every bus driver who ever existed was an asshole. We called 'em bustards, you know a cross between bastard and bus driver. Like, look at that bustard. Nothing better than leaning into the aisle to shoot the bus driver the finger when they weren't looking. Kids would hit each other, break each other's shit, practice new swear words or repeat the ones they already knew. It was like a jungle on wheels. In the winter, the it would fog up, and we'd draw cocks on the windows."

    That sounds terrible.

    "It wasn't so bad."

    You're kind of like my bus driver.

    "Don't you dare."

    Don't worry, you're not a total bustard.

    "I try."

Chapter 2: Paving the Broken Road

Ajax followed, feeling the absence of her compatriots for the first time. The Fury never sent Chicken Kickers out into the world on their own. She claimed the forces of chaos were too strong, that they were capable of corrupting even the most devout Chicken Kicker. Ajax was not worried. Of all the Kickers in her class, she was the one who had never strayed from the tenets of The Fury… until now. But it was for a good reason.

On her belly, she crawled through a field of grass, dogging the steps of the comedian. She moved at a quick pace, and she knew it would take some time for her to gain ground on him. In a tracking situation, the prey had the advantage; they could go wherever they wanted without having to study the ground for signs. Here, in this lush but deadly field, Ajax could track him easily. But she had done her homework. The maps of The Coop, marked and amended by a generation of Chicken Kickers, spoke of an impassable wasteland to the east of the coastal corridor.

The Fury told them not to go there. The wastes were too big, too deadly—too unpredictable. But Ajax wasn't scared, and though she agreed with The Fury on much, she didn't agree with her on this. If they wanted to pave the broken road, they had to go to it, not spend their lives paving that which was barely holding on.

The Fury, named after the mastermind behind the Avengers, and not for her horrible temper, would actually be furious with her if she knew Ajax had decided to go her own way. Though the comedian might seem harmless, and indeed, Comet and Silver seemed to think he was no worse than your typical morally-challenged waster, Ajax knew he was indicative of what was wrong with the world.

Ajax hearkened back to her lessons, hearkened back to the teachings of The Fury.

****

The branches of the apple tree hung heavy in the false fall, their twisted fruits, of which only perhaps twenty-percent of the flesh was edible, shone a sickly brownish-red in the glow of the burnt sky.

In front of the trees, The Fury stalked, her mace firmly grasped in her hands, her boots kicking up clouds of dust. The mace wasn't padded this time, and Ajax knew she was in for the beating of her life—if she let it happen.

The Fury, a woman slightly shorter than Ajax, who had reached her full height early on in life, came at her, a scowl on her face. Ajax knew if she stood and took the beating, it would be over quick, but if she fought back, well, it would only end when one of them was unconscious or broken.

Her teacher's arm raised into the air, too high, easy to read. Those who could take the beating, were filled with order. They were ready to pave the broken road.

As the arm came down, Ajax dodged out of the way, and The Fury spun, lashing out at her with the mace. It swept across her ribs, and the would-be warrior landed on the ground, amazed at how quickly The Fury moved. For someone who didn't go out into the world, she fought like a veteran of many battles, which she was. The Coop and its warriors had paved the broken roads in the surrounding area years ago. The raiders, once a menace, had been decimated, their leaders' heads placed on pikes at the outer edge of The Coop's land where the little ones would not see them. *They must be protected from Rated-R at all costs.*

But Ajax was no child. She had graduated from G to PG to PG-13, and now she was ready for the world. And

28

it was the world that made her fight back, to resist the benign punishment of The Fury.

She wanted to experience the R-Rating. She wanted to swim in the Deadpool, with Thorn if she was lucky. But if she took the beating, she wouldn't walk for a week.

As Ajax lashed out, the steel pipe of her mace clanged off the haft of The Fury's weapon. Her teacher cracked Ajax across the ribs, sending a rush of air exploding from her lungs. The Fury's face contorted, and she lashed out with her boot, sweeping Ajax's legs out from underneath her. The grizzled warrior raised her foot in the air, and the heel of that boot was aimed directly at her face. Somewhere in the back of her mind, the young woman registered the pain of her broken ribs as she rolled out of the way, and she realized there was something more to this fight than a potential Kicker challenging The Fury.

"What are you doing?" Ajax gasped.

"Your pavement isn't set. You're not ready, and I'll show you that."

The Fury swung at her, and Ajax lifted her mace in a blocking pattern known as Rose's Watch. She spun and danced away.

"I'm the best fighter in my class!" she spat.

The Fury leveled cold blue eyes at Ajax and growled. Their fight, meant to be nothing more than a simple disciplinary meeting for engaging in PG-13 talk around the little ones, had turned into something more. Her peers Silver and Comet stood to the side, their faces perfect pictures of impartiality. Others were present as well, Banner, Kanada, and Thorn. Her face flushed red as she realized Thorn was there, watching.

"You can't even stay G in front of the little ones, and you think you're ready to bring order to chaos?"

Ajax lifted her mace. There was no argument she could make that would excuse her actions. Now, all she could do was fight, bring the justice and the order to The

Fury. For in might, there was order—this from The Fury's mouth herself.

She rushed, holding her mace like a baton. The Fury was fast, faster than anyone else her age, but she no longer had her youth. The Fury's speed was born of experience and purity of thought. Ajax's speed was born of youth. She swung at the haft of The Fury's mace, and with a great clang that vibrated her arm up to her shoulder, The Fury blocked her strike.

Before The Fury could pull away, Ajax wrapped her hand around the haft of her teacher's mace, and The Fury spat in her eyes. Blinded and shocked, she lost her grip on the mace, and then she was on the ground, her head ringing and pain exploding throughout her body as The Fury laid into her.

Then Cap was there, always the peacemaker in his red and blue sweater, dragging The Fury off of her. She would not make it to the Deadpool that night, nor for many nights after. By then, Kanada and Thorn had become a couple, and Ajax would hold it against The Fury for many winters after that.

She tried to forgive her mother, to be as loving as Dorothy was to Sophia, despite her many obvious shortcomings. Mothers were mothers after all, even if they were The Fury. But her hate would become part of her own internal order, her own system of being, which according to the teachings at The Coop were the basis of paving the broken road.

****

Most Chicken Kickers would have turned back as soon as the comedian had turned east to set out across the wastes. But not Ajax. She had always gone her own way. Not because she was stubborn, but because she knew there were paths through the waste, paths where she could do more good than just scouring villages for thieves and lowlifes. The wastes were where the real work needed to be done.

Her foot bumped into something dense and squishy at the same time. She looked down to behold a pitiful sight, some creature, some woodland thing had been skinned and eaten raw. *Was it the comedian? Did he feed like a beast when the situation presented itself?* If so, he was further gone than she suspected. Perhaps he was a Loki, a shapeshifting troublemaker capable of being nice and gentlemanly when the means justified the ends. But at his heart, a Loki was a damaged piece of shit. Better to be put down than to have to live with the fear of that transformation. A Loki always turned, and so too would the comedian, unless she could stop him.

As the green spaces gave way to the brown, and the waste fog closed in, Ajax continued her trek. She didn't want to be out in the open. Not at night. It would be impossible to track him in the darkness, and she was only one person. On top of that, she did not know the way of the wastes, only what she had heard in stories. She would have to find a place to sleep soon.

Chapter 3: Evercrack

The world stood on the verge of sun-up when the earth tried to kill him for the millionth time. The comedian, anxious to finish his quest, to lay hands on Cheatums Sterling, lay on the floor of the bus remembering what it had once been like to ride in the cheese wagon, to wake up early, before the buttcrack of dawn, pack up all your shit and collapse into the pleathery bench seat of the bus, with its windows fogging and old Carl Grier cracking racist jokes in the back, despite the fact he would never do so to a kid's face. That's one rule the comedian followed. If he wasn't willing to say a joke to an audience's face, he certainly wouldn't say it behind their back. Unfortunately, for him, there was very little he wouldn't say to an audience's face. But racist shit, that was for the lowest of the low. In the grand scheme of things, a racist was worse than a raider, especially now when life was in such short supply, human life at least. They were all the same, sad smudges trudging along a spinning ball that treated them like an infection. It didn't matter what color your skin was anymore—never had.

He was constructing a hierarchy of wasteland society, with himself at the top of course, and the raiders at the bottom, when he felt the bus rock gently from side to side.

The comedian didn't wait. Hesitation was death. He hopped to his boots, the memory of trying to figure out where to slot merchants in the hierarchy (low) already vanished from his mind. He grabbed his bag, already neatly packed, and slung it over one shoulder even as the ground began to quake more violently. It did that from time to time. Apparently, hundreds of nuclear explosions around the globe had a way of antagonizing the earth and its tectonic plates. That's what the few remaining scientists had

32

said before the TV had gone dead. Of course, what did scientists know? They couldn't predict how quickly the world would fall or how quickly man would shed the comforts of civilization for a jar of marshmallow fluff, so what did they really know in the end?

The bus rocked from side to side now, and he knew he had to escape. With his sword in hand, he scooped up the tiny piano off the ground and pounded for the front doors. The ground tilted this way and that, and the closer he came to the front doors of the bus, the more the ground bucked, as if it were trying to throw him off balance, prevent him from escaping. It was then the fear hit him. *Maybe it's not just an earthquake. Maybe it's something more.*

The windows on the bus shattered, and from above, he heard the piercing call of the shrieker. It was close now, hovering only thirty-feet in the air, drawn by the groaning steel and shattered glass of the bus. The comedian's ears rang from the concussive blast of the shriek, and it was a miracle he managed to stay on his feet. He didn't know if the windows broke because of the bus's shaking or because of the power of the shrieker's scream. Like an old man experiencing the first signs of an oncoming bout of explosive diarrhea, he needed to get the fuck off the bus.

He hit the doors, throwing his shoulder into them, but their rusty stubbornness won out. He thrust the tips of his fingers through the small crack between the bus doors and the door frame, and he pushed with all of his weight. The door accordioned open with a squeal only slightly quieter than the shrieker's call.

Knowing he wasn't out of the proverbial woods yet, he didn't dive to the ground, but sprinted from the bus. His grunts, his strains, the squeal of the bus doors opening, all of these would mean one thing to the shrieker. Time to feed.

As he ran further and further from the bus, the shaking of the earth subsided, though it did not stop altogether. Above, the shrieker called again, and this time, the comedian took the full blast of its horrible yell. His brains were scrambled in an instant, but he had the presence of mind to stop, drop, and roll. The shrieker thumped into the ground where he had been, and its leathery wings battered him. Deadly talons like a tiger's teeth dotted the outer edge of its wings. With a puff of dust and a thunderous clap, the creature launched into the air. It preferred to dive, strike, and drag its prey into the air where it would rip its belly open with the talons on its feet.

It knew it could be beat on the ground. It was smart. It should be; those who had seen them up close swore shriekers had once been human. The comedian pulled a couple of tufts of dead grass from the parched soil, rolled them between his fingers, and managed to stuff them in his ears before the shrieker dove again, letting loose another brain-shredding screech. This time, he was able to keep his wits about him, and he pulled his massive sword free. He stood like a hitter waiting on a 90 mile-per-hour fastball. As the shrieker came on, its eyeless, bald head looking like the tip of a bowling pin wrapped in crinkled brown leather, he stepped to the side and swung the sword. The blade, though not the sharpest, relied mostly on its weight and size to do damage, and this it did gloriously. The shrieker's pitiful wing tore apart like newspaper, and black blood speckled the ground.

Behind him, the ground underneath the bus shook once more, and the comedian lost his balance for a moment. The wounded creature flopped on the earth, the talons of its one good wing swinging wildly to connect with the comedian. He skipped out of the way and squatted on his haunches, examining the creature from a safe distance. Most of what he had heard about shriekers had come secondhand, wasteland legends whispered in shitty cantinas

34

where they drank homemade corn whiskey. In the tales he'd heard, the shriekers had first appeared far to the east, on the other side of the Appalachian Mountains.

They had emerged from caves, old coal mines that had been converted into makeshift fallout shelters. Most stories agreed about that. The one thing they couldn't agree on was whether or not the shriekers were the results of irradiated, inbred humans living in darkness or if they were something those survivors had unleashed from the bowels of the earth. As the comedian studied the creature, its leather head searched back and forth, a tongue snaking out through teeth that looked like something you might find on a jack-o'-lantern, sharp, pointy, and numerous.

"Hey, ugly," he whispered.

Didn't your mother ever tell you not to torture animals? Oddrey asked.

"Shut up. I'm learning," he whispered.

The creature turned in his direction and charged, awkward and clumsy like a newly hatched chick. Just to be sure, the comedian swung his sword at the other wing. The bones in its wings were pathetically thin. At the end of the wing, the bones spread out into a long-fingered hand like a pterodactyl he had once seen in a museum with… with no one in particular.

Its genitals were small, withered things, but they were mostly human-like. The creature, now about as dangerous as a wild turkey, hopped on its taloned feet.

Two-hundred feet to the comedian's left, the earth opened up. The dirt underneath the bus disappeared, as did the rocks, the soil, and the plants. The bus itself was the last thing to tumble into the hole. The shrieker, convinced its prey was in that direction, gave blind chase. The comedian didn't stop him. Whether it had been human or not, it had tried to kill him, so he let the hairless, leathery monstrosity run straight for the gaping hole that had opened in the earth. Just as it reached the point of no return, he yelled, "Have a nice trip!" The creature spun and turned its half-severed wing flailing in the air, but it was too late. It plummeted into the pit and the comedian ran to the edge.

He found the creature hanging by the end of its spindly hand, the webbing of its wingtip impaled on a spike of rock. A shining gleam caught his eye, and when he looked at the elongated digit of its pterodactyl hand, he saw something there that made his blood curdle—a wedding ring. Jokes ran through his head, set-ups and punchlines spinning like reels on a slot machine. He pulled the plug on that machine and knelt next to the creature. It shrieked, and even through the wadded grass stuffed in his ears, he felt the pain of its screams.

"I'm sorry this happened to you." Then he reached out with trembling hands and pulled the wing from the rock. Its weight sent the shrieker plummeting forever into the green eldritch light that filtered up from the depths of the earth.

This was no ordinary chasm. The creature would not fall to the bottom and have its life mercifully ended. It was an evercrack, a bottomless pit. The first had appeared soon after the earthquakes. After that, they spread across the globe. The scientists, upon discovering their first one, had sent probe after probe into its depths and none had ever come back. As for the green light that issued forth, it was unexplained so far. As the world continued to die and continued to split, the evercracks became another inexplicable part of the landscape.

The bus had fallen some time ago, had fallen at least five minutes before the shrieker. If there was a bottom, he would have heard it by now. These cracks turned everything people knew about the world on end, stood it on its side. That poor creature... it would tumble forever.

Maybe he should have let it kill him, let it take his life from him. *What right do I have to live? I'm a human.*

36

I'm just as responsible for all this fucked up shit as anybody else. I'm not a cure. I'm a part of the disease, a virus walking.

It was then he really stared into the pit, tried to see to the bottom of it. The shifting light of the evercrack reminded him of when he was a child, and he would dive to the bottom of the pool to get away from the commotion of the other children. The sunlight filtering through the jiggling water would filter down just as the emerald light filtered up from the crack now. *Maybe I'm at the bottom of the pool, and if I step into that crack, I'll wind up somewhere else, somewhere where the sun shines and children play.*

He didn't know how long he stood there, licking his lips and peering into the depths of the crack trying to see a bottom that didn't exist. The evercracks were good, a humane way for people to end their lives. Maybe... maybe you'd just float forever until you starved to death.

Crack kills, a small voice said.

Half-heartedly, he asked Oddrey, "Did you see a plumber somewhere?"

I don't know what a plumber is.

"You know. One of the Mario Brothers."

Oddrey fell silent, and he was alone with his misery, the gift of the pit just a step away.

"What do you think's down there, Odd?"

Not what you're looking for.

The comedian wondered if maybe the evercrack was exactly what he was looking for. There's exhaustion, which the comedian felt, and then there's soul sickness. A quick nap can help with exhaustion... soul sickness though—once a sickness got to your soul, it was all over. He tried to peer into his own being, examine his state through unclouded eyes. *Am I sick? Am I ready to end it?*

The comedian's stomach grumbled. His lips were dryer than a desert rock at high noon. "Ah, fuck it. I hate being hungry."

With that, he turned and walked away from the pit.

You wouldn't have taken me with you, would you?

"Are you kidding? Where I go, you go. We're a team."

Odd fell silent then. The comedian turned around once, glancing back at the evercrack. He shrugged, shouldered his gear, and prepared for another stomach grumbling, terrifying day in the apocalypse. There would be more cracks, more opportunities if he so wished, but he wasn't done yet. He still had business on this broken, dying earth.

Casting a glance at the ground, he spotted the severed, leathery wing of the shrieker. "You think it tastes like jerky?"

Don't eat that.

"I mean—a little nibble couldn't hurt, just to fill the void."

Isn't that cannibalism?

"I call it survival."

It looks tough. Not a lot of meat on those skinny bones, and you don't know what turned him into a shrieker.

"Good lord, listen to district attorney Odd over here, makin' her case! Fine. Fine. I won't eat it. But I don't want to hear you complain when I gripe about being hungry."

Deal.

With that, the comedian resumed his journey. With each step away from the evercrack, his mind clouded over as if the waste mist existed in his brain as well. Within a few minutes, he forgot how close he had come to killing himself and taking Odd with him. He would never hurt Oddrey.

Chapter 4: Kickin' a Chicken

Ajax chewed half-heartedly on a Twizzler with the consistency of vulcanized rubber. She had plucked it free from a cupboard in an old apartment complex. With her own supplies not as robust as she might have wished, she had taken the time to search the apartment complex from top to bottom, surprised to discover the comedian had left some good stuff behind. A stash of candy underneath a child's bed in a locked apartment was providing her with some quick energy, though her mouth stung with the tang of battery acid from the chemically concocted confections. Twizzlers always did that.

After scouring the apartment complex, she had feasted on the candy, saving some for later. That quick-burst fuel allowed her to jog through the wasteland for a short time. Confident she was gaining ground, she didn't mind the extra expenditure of energy. Then she heard the sound of the shrieker in the distance.

She had no experience with the creatures, only the knowledge the other Chicken Kickers had brought back with them in their travels. Needless to say, she did not want to run afoul of a shrieker. Once she heard the first supersonic bellow, she slowed to a walk, hoping the shrieker wouldn't catch the comedian before she did. If that happened, then her mission would be over, and the wasteland and all its wonders, good and bad, would be lost to her. Without a mission, she would need to go home. That, or she would never be allowed to return home again.

A Chicken Kicker who did not act with purpose was merely another agent of chaos, and once you succumbed to chaos, there was no place in The Coop for you. Though she longed to see and explore, if she had no mission, she would return home as she had been trained to do.

She chiseled off another chunk of Twizzler, her teeth clicking together as she finally managed to slice through the rope of pure sugar. It dissolved in her mouth slowly and tasted like nothing more than a combination of sugar and food dyes.

What I wouldn't give for some good old-fashioned chicken. Besides the people, it was the one thing she really missed about The Coop. Say what you will about the place, but Coop chicken was the best meal in the wasteland, as far as she could tell. It certainly put the Twizzler on which she gnawed to shame.

The only problem with the chickens back home was how mouthy they were. No one knew when the chickens developed the ability to talk, but once they did, wrestling eggs from them became quite the chore. As a youth, she, along with the others of her age, had been tasked with collecting eggs in the chicken coop. It was another part of their training. While the entire place was referred to as The Coop, for those who lived there, the actual chicken coop stood on the edge of the property.

According to her mother and the other grayhairs back home, chickens didn't used to be able to talk at all. They used to just walk around saying "buck buck." And the things these chickens said—well, let's just say that's there's a reason her order was known as the Chicken Kickers.

****

On their first day in the coop, Comet and Ajax walked the rows of the chicken shack with buckets in their hands. The boots on their feet were comically large, but Howard, the man in charge of the chicken coop, assured them if they kept training, they would both fill them out nicely in a year or two.

All around them, chickens sat babbling on a three-tiered row of racks. "Do you have an egg under you?" Ajax asked one chicken.

"No. I haven't laid one yet. Come back tomorrow," the chicken squawked. Chicken voices were loud, obnoxious, and Ajax put this down to them not being all that bright. Despite this fact, they still tried to trick the children tasked with collecting eggs.

"Any luck over there?" Ajax asked Comet, her closest friend.

"Nope."

They continued down the rows, asking chicken after chicken if they had laid an egg, but the answer was always the same. When they returned to Howard and explained the situation, he scoffed at them, almost breaking into some PG-13 language which would have gotten him a visit from The Fury, for they were not yet old enough for PG-13 content.

He crooked a finger at them and had them follow him back into the coop. He leaned against one of the metal racks, real nonchalant like.

"Hey there, Chicken. You got an egg under there?"

"Nope. No eggs here," the chicken said.

"What's your name?" Howard asked.

"Howard."

"No way! That's my name."

"No, it's not."

Howard tossed a smug look at the two girls in their huge rubber boots. "Check this out," whispered to them. "What type of an animal are you?"

"I'm a frog."

"But frogs don't lay eggs!"

"Yes, they do! See?" The chicken raised up, and underneath was a large brown egg. Howard snatched it away from the chicken and then walked it over to the girls. Comet held out her wire basket, and the man, with a pleased smile upon his face, placed the egg gently in the bottom.

"Do you get it now?"

Comet nodded her head.

Howard tapped Ajax hard in the middle of her forehead with a dirty index finger. "What about you? Your mother always said you were sort of hard-headed."

"I don't understand why we don't just take the eggs."

Howard beamed at her.

"Well, little one. These are our friends. If you make your friends unhappy, what happens?"

"They stop being your friends?"

"Bingo!"

Howard leaned in close. "On top of that, anyone with half a brain can get what they want using physical violence. Look at the raiders out there. They're stupid as shhh—shillings. But we want you to be smarter than that. Get it?"

Ajax nodded. She was beginning to understand.

"Now, if you can't trick an egg from a chicken, what chance are you going to have out there in the real world once you run into something with more than a chicken brain?"

"Not much."

"Not much at all," Howard agreed. "Now try it out. And if you can get an egg from Einstein down there, there's a special prize for ya."

Comet and Ajax shared a look, and then it was a race to get to Einstein, with Ajax interrogating the chickens on the right and Comet harassing the chickens on the left.

"Hello, chicken," Ajax said to the next fowl in line.

"I'm no chicken."

"Then what are you?"

"I'm you!"

"You're not me. I'm me."

Ajax, looked over her shoulder to find Howard leaning back in his chair, one leg crossed over the other as he whittled a piece of wood into the best Eye of Agomotto in The Coop. From the corner of her eye, she saw Comet proceed to the next chicken, another egg rattling around in her basket.

Ajax turned to look at the chicken. "If you're me, then why are you sitting?"

"I'm not sitting!" the chicken announced, fully outraged, and then it stood. Ajax snatched the egg as quickly as she could, receiving a small peck on the wrist for her trouble.

On and on the two went, racing and competing to be the first one to reach Einstein. If the prize was a hand-carved, Howard-crafted Eye of Agamotto, then it was a prize she had to have. The others would be deliciously jealous of her if she possessed one of those. On the flipside, she would never forgive Comet if she won.

While she had once respected the chickens in the coop, as most children did since they offered eggs and the occasional meat, she soon found herself loathing them. Their stupidity was ubiquitous, and their incessant need to lie was always their undoing. They could talk, so she had assumed they were intelligent, but they were anything but. She had seen toads with more intelligence.

At first, she had felt bad taking their eggs from them, but the chickens didn't complain a bit about it. Once an egg was taken, they returned to talking to their neighbors about this and that, as if the egg had been forgotten completely. They engaged in all forms of gossip about each other, and even about Howard. "Oh, did ya hear about Madge? She caught her best friend with the rooster she had her eye on, in the field no less."

On and on the chickens babbled, never seeming to realize the peril they were in. At any moment, someone could come in here, pick one of them up and take them out to the chopping block, but they blathered without pause while Comet and Ajax tricked them into showing themselves guilty. It began to feel unfair to Ajax, these chickens, fighting so hard to protect the only thing they owned, only to be entrapped by the devious questioning of two eight-year-old humans.

But in the end, they were chickens, and she was the human, and what a chicken asked for is exactly what a chicken got. If they were going to lie and hide their eggs, then this is how it had to be.

On that first day, Ajax was disappointed to find Comet at the end stall, grilling Einstein, the smartest chicken of the bunch.

"Have you seen the weather outside?" Comet asked.

"I plead the Fifth."

"What's the Fifth?" Comet asked.

"I plead the Fifth," the chicken repeated.

Comet turned to Ajax and shrugged her soldiers. "Does that make any sense to you?"

Ajax shook her head, and as she finished collecting the last egg from her own row, she said, "Let me give it a shot." She strode to the end of the chicken shack, and there, on its own pedestal, sat the largest chicken she had ever laid eyes on. Twice the size of the other chickens, it regarded her with reptilian eyes. "What's your name?" she asked.

"I plead the Fifth."

For hours, the two girls went back and forth, trying to trick Einstein into saying something else besides "I plead the Fifth." The air in the coop became stuffy as the sun rose overhead, and the smell of chicken shit began to make Ajax's head swim. All around her, the babble of the chickens went on and on, a nonstop cavalcade of "Didjahears" and "Didjaknows" creating a river of gossip that made Ajax feel like she was becoming dumber just by hearing it.

"Just gimme the egg!" Comet shouted, and as she reached under Einstein's feathers it lashed out at her with a feisty beak and flesh-ripping talons.

44

"Ouch!" Comet called.

"Here let me help you." Ajax darted her hands under the chicken and received the same treatment.

Behind them, someone cleared their throat. It was Howard, standing with his arms crossed. "You're gonna lose a finger if you keep testing her."

"Well, what are we supposed to do then?" Comet whined.

Ajax could feel the prized Eye slipping away.

"Listen, there's a reason we have you kids collect these chicken eggs. Because we want you to see how simple people are."

"But these aren't people," Ajax said.

"You'd be surprised what the people outside of The Coop are like. And to be honest, I'd take these chickens any day. For most people, a good conversation is enough, but for some people, well, you just can't tell them a darn thing. You can talk to Einstein until you're blue in the face, and all she's ever going to do is plead the Fifth."

"What even is the fifth?" Comet asked.

"Don't you worry about it. It's just one of those things in the past that led us to all this in the first place."

Howard guided the children backward and stepped up between them. "Now, when you're out there, among all the clucking chickens, who always lie by the way, you may encounter one of these people who doesn't want to tell you anything. Maybe they're a raider. Maybe they're a psycho who likes to eat little children such as yourselves." He giggled like a comical madman, and Ajax found herself smiling at his antics. "In that case, there's only one thing to do with 'em."

Howard turned and spun on his heel, one of his legs arcing up. The tip of his boot thumped into Einstein's posterior, and with a squawk and a ruffle of feathers, it shot into the air.

45

"Sometimes, you just have to kick a chicken to make it see the light." Howard reached into Einstein's vacated nest and plucked out an orange-brown egg. "See?"

****

She could almost see the egg in her mind. As the sun hovered overhead, she recalled holding eggs up to the sun to see if she could detect a chicken inside.

As the past melted away, she lowered her eyes and continued trudging through the mist. In time, a building loomed out of the charred fog, square and unassuming. The sign on the front door said "Midday Cheese Factory." Always cautious, she did a lap around the building, mimicking the comedian's footsteps. The warehouse was a dead thing, a last crumbling sign of order among the wastes. Its concrete walls and broken glass windows filled her with melancholy. It would have made a nice home for someone.

She kicked at the dry, dusty topsoil of the apocalypse, and a puff of grit floated through the air. That soil wouldn't allow a single beet to grow. It was sick and dying like the rest of the world. Chaos was having its way out here, unchecked.

Rather than step into the cheese factory and toil among the memories of the dead, she found the comedian's tracks walking away from the building. This was one way to gain ground on him, though it meant missing out on some potentially delicious cheese. She had eaten cheese in the past, goat's cheese, in the place she had lived in before The Coop.

Though she had been young, she still remembered the mischievous eyes of Ms. Geit, the old family goat. This was when she lived with her real mother and her real father, two people she only barely remembered.

****

A small wind swirled the tips of the freshly cropped grass. Ms. Geit munched calmly next to her, nibbling the longer blades. Sometimes, Ajax would walk over and pet the goat on her swollen sides as she stared deep into her almost human eyes.

Her father was inside the barn, tending to the tools, which he did by feel. His eyes had been burned out by the bombs. It seemed all her parents talked about was the bombs and the world before they came.

Ajax had no memory of that world. She had been too young to remember the world before, but her parents assured her she would see it once more, even if it took a while.

She was petting Ms. Geit when a sharp scream came from the barn. It sounded like a scream of pain, and she huddled in the grass, holding onto one of Ms. Geit's legs. She didn't seem to mind. All she wanted to do was eat grass and be left alone.

From the barn, two men emerged, skinny, their eyes mean. Where they weren't covered in blood, their weapons were shiny and metallic. They went inside the house and there were more screams, her mother's this time. It was then she ran as her father had told her to do.

She heard her father's voice in her head, "If you ever see a stranger, you run. Doesn't matter how far you go, we'll find you. But shouldn't no one be comin' up this way, so if you see someone, they shouldn't be here. That means get out."

And so she had run, Ms. Geit following along with her. Wherever she went, Ms. Geit went, and for a while, Ajax was alone in the world with only a goat for a friend. She kept moving, until her shoes wore off her feet, and then she sat down in the dirt, waiting for her mother and father to find her. But someone else did first.

He was a man, red-bearded and large. He stank of leather and unwashed hair. The hair on his head was gray and tied in a ponytail.

He smiled at first, and even back then, Ajax knew it was a fake smile. He didn't have the face for smiles.

"C'mere, girl," the man had said.

Ajax had no intention of doing any such thing.

The man, displeased by her disobedience, stepped toward her, and Ms. Geit charged at the stranger, hitting him in the groin with the crown of her very hard skull. The man crumpled into the dust, and Ms. Geit stomped on his face until he stopped moving.

When she began to feed on the dead man, Ajax dragged her away, and together, they continued their journey. It was then she realized father hadn't been teaching Ms. Geit to dance, but to protect her.

Eventually, they would make their way to The Coop, where her new mother would adopt her and treat her as her own child. Ms. Geit, capable of producing milk, was welcomed into The Coop as well. Ajax would visit her every day until her death, and when Ms. Geit lay down and breathed her last breath, she wouldn't let the Chicken Kickers turn her into stew. She demanded they bury her, which they did.

****

She thought about Ms. Geit a lot, about her strength and quiet acceptance of the world. On the back of her one leather glove, she had embroidered a sigil of a goat. This goat was with her all the time, brought her power and strength. As Ajax moved deeper into the wastes, she knew these attributes would be needed.

The mists closed in around her, and the Midday Cheese Factory disappeared behind her, gobbled up by the mist. Still, she walked onward, calling on Ms. Geit to guide her as she had done when she was young and lost, even though she could still see the comedian's footsteps easily enough.

The worst thing about the wastes wasn't that anything could happen at any time; it was that for so much of the time, absolutely nothing happened. Not a damn thing. So far, the only thing exciting had been stumbling across a couple of abandoned buildings. Other than that, it was a whole lot of walking.

My luck can't be this good. Surely, something terrible should have happened to her by now. These were the forbidden wastes after all. With each step, she reminded herself of this fact, tried to keep herself tight and ready for danger. As soon as you let your guard down in the wastes, it would be over. The wastes had a dark sense of humor according to the elder Kickers who had ventured into the blasted landscape.

On and on she walked, wondering what she was going to do when she encountered the comedian. Would he fight her? Would he own up to his crimes? In the end, he would be dealt with. Order demanded it.

The miles paraded by, and the sand of the wastes found its way into every nook and cranny of her body. When the wind whipped, grit scratched across her eyes and flew up her nose. Even when the wind didn't blow, each boot step sent up a puff of dust that managed to work its way into her calf-length boots.

The sun baked Ajax from above, beating down upon her and turning her skin pink. Though it was warm in the wastes, it wasn't as hot as it could be. Still, she was forced to pull her hood up to combat the burning rays of the sun. Too much exposure to the sun could kill you as surely as a group of raiders. Already the skin of her nose stung, and she was forced to walk with her head down. When she needed to scan the horizon, she stopped and pulled her hood back, scanning quickly before covering back up. Her

49

skin was fair, too pale to withstand the sun for long. The comedian wouldn't have that problem. His skin was darker than hers, capable of handling the sun for longer periods of time.

As the miles stretched on, she resisted the urge to run. Moving faster than an easy, sweatless walk was suicide out here. Her own body was her enemy now. In the back of her mind, she began to imagine the time when her water would run out. It wouldn't be long now. Maybe a day or two. But dammit, she wanted to gain ground on the comedian.

She spotted the glow from the evercrack first, an eldritch light shooting into the air not unlike the dancing green of the radioactive heavens on a clear night. The radiance shifted and danced, and she found herself drawn to it, which was fortunate, because the comedian's path led in the same direction.

As she approached, she felt something calling to her, as if the light itself could speak.

She tried to remember what the elder Kickers said about evercracks, for they were not unknown to them. *Bottomless pits. Green light. A call that wormed its way into your mind and soul.* Part of her wanted to leave, the cautious part, the orderly part of her mind. *Turn around. It's not worth it.*

But the chaotic part of herself wanted to see, for all humans were a continuum of chaos and order battling within. At the edge of the pit, she spotted a leathery wing, as wide as she was tall, lying in the dust, and she realized she hadn't seen or heard the shrieker for some time. She squatted next to the wing, stopping short of touching it with her hands. The claw at the end of the wing looked vaguely human, and on the end of it, she spotted a twinkle in the sunlight. She removed her knife to carve at the flesh, careful not to touch the rotting meat of the shrieker's wing.

50

In the wastes, it was better to touch nothing. This came from an old man, Honey Badger, who despite the sweet moniker, was as cantankerous a man as she had ever seen. To prove his point, he had held out his right hand, which resembled a chunk of clay that was halfway through being molded into the shape of a human hand. "This was from a waste rose, as pretty a flower as you'll ever set eyes on. That's what I get for liking flowers." The blob of shapeless skin that had once been his nose was further proof.

The tip of her knife probed at the skin around the shrieker's claw, and eventually, she was able to uncover a circular metal band, like those she had seen in movies. A chill crawled up her spine as the implications of that metal band dawned on her. Shriekers had been human.

Superstition stole over her, as if the very thought of uncovering the shrieker's secrets could call another one out of the woodwork. She scanned the sky nervously, but it remained empty.

Ajax stood and studied the marks in the dusty ground, trying to put the pieces together. She wasn't much of a tracker; that had always been Comet's gift, but she knew there had been a fight here. She traced its progress to the edge of the pit. The green light called her, begged her to step closer to the edge of the abyss. With a hesitance in her steps, she did so.

She saw the tracks, saw the impressions on the edge of the pit, and knew something had gone into the hole. She stood a foot away from the precipice. *Worst thing about an evercrack,* a voice said in her mind, *is that they always grow. When you stand on the edge of one, you're playing with your life.*

Still, she needed to see. Her lower back complained as she bent forward, still maintaining enough tension in her body that she could leap backward if needed. As her face broke the circumference of the evercrack's edge, she felt

51

the green light wash over her cheeks, felt it as a small tingling that made her want to giggle a bit. The light pushed upward from the depths of the earth pressing gently against her skin like a lover's kiss. *Pure chaos. It's pure chaos.*

In the pit, she beheld the sides of the crack, ancient tree roots and rocks jutting from its edges. The middle of the evercrack swirled with green light, emerald in nature, and she thought she could hear the light calling to her. *Come down here,* it said. *Come be forever.* Even worse, around her boots, she felt something, like when you stood ankle deep in a stream and the weak current tries its best to sweep you off your feet. At the edge of the evercrack, she felt an unseen tide, and she wondered what was being sucked into the evercrack. *Hope? Time? Life itself?*

Through sheer will, she managed to pull away from the crack. She turned her back on the green light, squeezed her eyes shut, and shook her head to clear her mind. Still, the song of the light continued in her mind, assuring her everything would be alright if she but stepped into the void.

Pushing the song of the light to the back of her mind, she scanned the dirt, and there, she found the by now familiar outline of the comedian's boots. They strode away from the evercrack, dragging unsure footprints. They stopped and turned a few times on their way away from the crack, as if the comedian had also heard the song of the light and almost given in. But eventually, the tracks led away, and the further away from the pit the comedian went, the surer his footsteps were.

If he had been injured in his battle with the shrieker, he didn't show it.

He defeated a shrieker, something no one at The Coop had ever done... no one that had ever returned anyway. She filed the information away. If the comedian could kill a shrieker, then he would be a deadly opponent indeed.

52

Chapter 5: Ramen Shaman

The rocky border of the wastes gave way to a sandy, sunblasted environment that shouldn't exist. All traces of green eradicated, replaced by brown, stunted plants and shrubs that were more dangerous than the moisture-sucking desert itself. Whenever one of these plants popped up in the comedian's path, he wisely circled around it.

The waste mist thinned here, as if it wanted travelers to behold the emptiness of this stretch of the waste's barren landscape and despair. *Take a look,* the wastes seemed to say. *Behold the nothing. This is what is in store for you if you don't turn back now.*

The warning went unheeded by the comedian. He had been ignoring warnings for years, and at this point, his only hope was to move forward. His supplies were dangerously low. Even greater than food was his need for water.

His feet baked inside of his boots, and every step seemed to require a Herculean amount of effort. If he had brought a hundred gallons of water with him, he doubted he could slake the thirst he felt now.

His goggled eyes scanned the horizon, hoping for any sign of civilization, or for the corpse of Cheatums Sterling. As far as survivors went, Cheatums was one of the best. Despite his obvious shortcomings, he had managed to survive in the apocalypse when many hadn't. But this waste—there was no way Cheatums could make it through this on his own. Cheatums was a parasite. Without other humans to feed upon, he would have died a long time ago. Maybe he was already dead. He'd find out in Ike he supposed.

In the haze, he spotted something, a dark smudge on the horizon, nestled in the crotch of two hills that formed a small valley. Blinking his eyes and swiping at the sweat of his brow, he squinted to try and make out the shapes at the limits of his eyesight.

Just as he was about to figure it out, he stumbled over something buried in the sand. He fell face first, his gasping mouth scooping up hot grit. He let the sand sit in his mouth, as to spit it out would cost him precious moisture. Swallowing the sand, he rolled over to see what had tripped him up.

At his feet, a small white dome rose from the sand.

"Another fucking skull," he said, sand flying from his mouth as he spoke.

He swiped the back of a gloved hand across his lips to remove the fine granules, then dug furiously, plucking the child-size skull free, rage boiling hot in his chest. The skull was fleshless, either picked clean by scavengers or cooked bare by the blasted light of the sun.

Holding the skull level with his glare, the comedian peered into the empty eye sockets. "You following me?"

The skull's tiny teeth did not move.

It's just a skull, Oddrey said. *Seven billion people dead... you're bound to stumble across a few of these.*

"This isn't a different skull. It keeps following me."

The heat is getting to you.

"Nothing *gets* to me," the comedian said, tossing the skull into the sand for the next person to stumble over. As he rose to his feet, his boots made contact with several other objects buried in the sand. He kicked a few loose, uncovering a pile of the tiny skulls, some rib cages, a leg bone or two or three.

And then he realized he was sinking.

"No, no, no." He pushed his way upward, and the sand sucked at his body like a living thing, like a kid swirling a comedian-flavored Jolly Rancher around the inside of his mouth, but in the slowest, most indulgent of manners.

"Fuck."

Where his fingerless gloves touched the sand, his fingers came away singed and burnt. It was a small pain though. He looked out over the gritty expanse and realized he would have to cross it... the slow sand.

The shifting granules did not act quickly enough to trap the comedian completely. If he kept moving, he would be able to cross the shifting desert with no problem at all. But if he stopped, as these children had done, then he would be dead.

You could always go back, Oddrey said.

"Where's the fun in that?"

Better to be bored than dead.

"Says you," the comedian said as he stepped further into the slow sands. This time the dune swallowed his leg up to his knee, and he pushed forward like a man wading through deep, rushing water. He could feel the current of the sand pulling him downward, and he wondered what fresh horror awaited him in the desert's depths.

In the distance, he spotted the darkness between the two hills that jutted upward like the full breasts of a woman lying upon her back. He imagined them as such...

Pervert, Oddrey accused.

The comedian slogged onward, aware of the sweat pouring from his body as he worked his way across the sandy wastes. A faint breeze blew... downward, as if the very air itself were being sucked in by the sand. Perhaps that's why the waste fog was no longer present in this part of the world. Perhaps the sand had sucked it all down, inhaled it like a clover-smoker in a choke den.

How far do I have to go?

He tried to estimate the distance, but the clear air, clearer than anywhere else in the world as far as he knew, played tricks on his eyes. A mile, maybe two?

As he pressed forward, a noise registered in his ears, faint at first. He stopped in his tracks, the sand sucking on his boots and his shins. The interiors of his boots were heavy with desert, but it was of no concern at the moment. He slowed his labored breathing, and racked his brain to identify the strange sound in his ears—the sound of a hand rubbing across coarse beard stubble.

I don't like this, Oddrey said.

"You and me both." He took five steps forward, depriving the sand of a taste of his kneecap, and stopped to listen again once he had attained a satisfactory height. It seemed to him the rough, scraping noise came from multiple directions now, and panic took hold of his heart.

Then he spotted movement in the distance. Something thin, whip-like, scurried across the sand, heading straight for him. By its undulating movements, he knew it for a snake.

"Fucking sand snakes."

They came at a leisurely pace, and the comedian continued his march, for to stand still for too long would be a death sentence all its own. The knife in his hand was old, stained with blood, some of it his own, some of it not. He had used the knife for everything from killing raiders to shaving branches to creating kindling. Now he was going to use it to kill some motherfucking snakes.

Sensing more noise behind him, the comedian spun in a circle, his thighs burning from his journey through the sand. On they came, growing larger and larger as they sailed across the sand like schooners on the surface of the ocean. These were no ordinary snakes.

The sand ignored them as if they were nothing more than the wind crawling across the wavy dunes. Their wriggling bodies moved in time with each other, and it was then the comedian understood how all those skulls had come to be buried in the desert. Like spiders with a web, these snakes had adapted to the shifting sands mimicking the sound and feel of the wind.

Suddenly, the comedian was overcome by a sense of nostalgia for the early days of the apocalypse, when guns and ammunition had been readily available. A quick blast from his trusty AR-15 could have evened the odds here, turned those snakes into scale-covered pulp. But those were the old days, and all the good guns and all the good bullets had been used for bad things.

They reached him at the same time, and the comedian found himself in a battle for his life. His eyes grew wide behind his goggles, soaking up the information available to him. One of the snakes coiled up like a scaled poop emoji and lashed out at him. On instinct, his wrist flashed, and the first snake's head flew through the air, its mouth still open, the sun glinting off small beads of venom that dangled from its fangs.

He noted this only in passing, as he was too busy spinning counter-clockwise, always counter-clockwise. On his backswing, he caught another striking snake in his free hand and launched it through the air. As a third darted for his thigh, he brought the knife back close to his body, chopping downward, and severing its head, even as a fourth serpent struck him in the back. It struck like lightning, faster than he could spin, and he heard a dull thunk as its clear, translucent fangs clanged off the blade of his sword, deflecting what would surely have been a killing blow.

Dazed, the snake pulled back, its flexible body waving back and forth in the hot air, like a snake charmer... or a human charmer in this case. His free hand darted out and snatched the snake by the tail. In one smooth movement, he shot his arm out, cracking its body like a whip. The pure force of the comedian's movement sent the serpent's brains flying out its sensitive nostrils. He dropped the dead thing in the sand, where its tail twitched. Already the sand was claiming the bodies of the snakes, and the one he had thrown returned to take vengeance for its dead brethren.

The serpent, its head as big as one of his fists, stopped and stared at him, its tongue flicking out to taste the burnt air. The comedian stared back. He decided its eyes were demonic in nature. Smartly, it stayed out of range, flattening its body against the sand. They watched each other, snake and man, and doll head.

The sand rasped against his jacket as he sunk deeper into it, and he knew he would have to make the first move. If he waited, the sand would swallow him whole.

Don't do it, Oddrey said.

"Hey, snakeface. I got a joke for you."

The snake regarded him with those oddly intelligent eyes.

"Why is it so hard to fool a snake?"

Its forked tongue flicked out in response, as if to say, "Why?"

"Because they have no legs to pull."

If a snake could frown, this one did, and then it launched at the comedian, its mouth wide open. The comedian swung his arm, and the blade of Rib-Tickler, cut through its pellucid fangs, spraying spots of venom into the sand. The blade continued, slicing through the hinges of the snake's jaw, and its body flopped onto the sand.

When it finally stopped twitching, the comedian stood buried up to his belly button in warm sand.

Even snakes think you're not funny.

"Why should they be any different from anyone else?"

The comedian sheathed Rib-Tickler and then plucked the snake corpse from the sand before it was swallowed completely. He threw it over his shoulder like a coil of rope, and continued on his way, listening for the sound of a rough palm scraping across stubble.

****

58

At the edge of the shifting sand, the comedian stopped to take a revenge piss. As he undid his pants, he tried to shake out all the loose granules that had found their way into his stained underclothes, but he knew unless he fully disrobed, he would be finding sand grains for weeks.

Still, it felt mighty fine to piss on that sand.

You're going to get a sunburn, Oddrey said.

"Nah, just a healthy tan." He sighed as he finished and resumed his walk, his sand-coated thighs scraping against his pants.

The land on the other side of the slow sands was hilly, but at least it was good old-fashioned dirt, dry and dead. The hills he had seen in the distance rose up to his left and right, loose rocks piled around their bottom as the world tried to flatten those glorious mounds. Between the two hills, he spotted a tumbledown shack made of timbers that might have been as old as the hills themselves.

As he walked toward the shack, he spotted a small spark. At first, he thought he had absorbed too much sun, but then the spark came once more, and he knew someone was in the shack.

He eyed the hills to his sides, too steep and too barren to climb without becoming dehydrated. The sands behind him were also out of the question, as he had already wasted precious energy in making his way across it once.

Ahead then.

Yes. I'm a head, Oddrey said.

"No, not 'a head.' Ahead, you dingbat."

What's a dingbat?

"Funny you should ask."

The question's funny, but I bet the answer isn't.

"One day, you're gonna go solo, and you're gonna slay, Odd. I mean it. A dingbat is a symbol that you put in place instead of letters when you don't feel like spelling out a swear word."

Why the fuck would you do that?

59

"I don't fucking know. What do I look like, Encyclopedia Britannica?

What's that?

"Just shut up."

With his quads and calves no longer burning, he strode forward.

As he came within fifty paces of the wooden shack, he called out, "Greetings and salutations in there."

The only sound was that of absolute silence, which meant he had been heard.

"I come in peace. Killed all those snakes for ya. If you got something to drink, I got some meat."

A scrabbling came from the shack, and a small, wiry man peered out at him. His skin was dark, and his eyes were crazed. The curly hair on his head stuck out in all directions, defying gravity. "You real?" the man asked.

"Are any of us?"

"Am I real?"

"Not a philosopher, huh?" he muttered to himself. "Yeah. You're real, and I'm real. But most of all, this snake's real."

The man licked his dry lips. "Come on in. But no funny stuff."

I don't think he has to worry about that with you, Oddrey said.

"F@%$."

Oh. I get it now.

****

Though he didn't think it was possible, the interior of the shack was smaller than it looked from the outside. The boards were so gray as to be almost white, and he thought if he reached out to touch them, they would crumble to dust.

He sat cross-legged, patchouli-style on the ground. Across from him, the man did the same. His host had insisted he leave Side-Splitter outside, and he had done so, though he felt naked without it.

The snake's corpse sat between them, within easy reach of either man.

"Been a while since anyone come through the sands."

"I'm looking for a man."

"Well, it ain't gonna be me. I tried that once. Might be for some people, but it's not for me."

"No. Not like to... date. I'm looking for a specific man."

"Like I said, ain't no one been through here in a while."

"He would have been of medium height, has a face that seems attractive at first, but then you realize he's actually pretty ugly when you spend any time with him. Loves to gamble."

"Oh, yeah. That guy. He come through here about a week ago. Then the handsome lad came later."

"You just said no one's been here in a while."

"Well, a while is pretty relative. Not very specific at all."

"Speaking of relatives, did the second man look like he could have been a relative of the first?"

"I don't know. I'm blind."

"Is that why you live out in the middle of nowhere?"

"Huh? This ain't Atlanta?"

"Are you fucking with me?"

He's crazy. Just eat the snake and leave, Oddrey said.

"Nope. Last time I could see, I was in Atlanta."

"Well, this isn't Atlanta."

"Where is it?"

"I don't know. It's all relative these days."

"Yes, I do believe they were relatives."

"Did you talk to them? These men?"

The man scraped a hand across his stubbled jaw and said, "Yeah. Well, I talked to the first one, but he gambled me out of my last jug of water. Been waiting to go up to the store for a while. When the other one come around, I didn't feel like getting gambled out of my last treasure, so I laid low and let him pass."

The comedian's ears perked up. "A treasure?"

The man smiled at him, his yellow teeth shining in the firelight. Smoke filled the cabin, escaping through a hundred different exit points in the rickety walls. Suddenly, the man stood, and the comedian fought the urge to reach for his knife.

Scrabbling to a corner of the shack, the man began digging in the loose soil. When he turned around, he held out a plastic-wrapped fortune.

"Is that soy sauce flavor?"

The blind man smiled at him and gave an easy nod. He held the package with the reverence of a holy man holding a sacred text. Squatting next to the fire, the comedian's mouth watered. He would chop off a finger just to have the sauce packet inside. He could live for a week off that one block of ramen.

"You want some of this?" the blind man said.

"I don't have anything valuable enough to offer for that."

"A man is a fortune unto himself."

He wants sex, Oddrey said.

The comedian, in silent agreement, waited for the man to make his move.

"You have more value than you know."

"I'm a comedian, the most worthless thing in the world."

"But you're also a human. You've seen things. You've lived. I've been in my shack for years, waiting to share this ramen with someone worthy of it."

"Years? You can't have been here for years."

The man's yellow-toothed smile went crooked. "You don't know, do you?"

"Don't know what?"

"About the world."

"There's not much to know."

"Your time is your time. My time is my time. What seems an hour to you, is a year for me. Already, I've known you for months. Know you better than my own brother, bless his soul."

"Months. Ha."

"I'm sorry about your loss. Do you want to share it with me?"

The comedian suddenly had the urge to rise and leave. His head spun, and the smoke from the fire seemed—different, as if something extra floated among the charred wood particles.

"I'll share the ramen, but my loss is mine."

"I knew you'd say that."

"What am I going to say next?"

"You're going to leave."

"Ha! I'm planning on staying right here."

"But, then you'll leave." The blind man patted the package of ramen. "Come, we cook the snake, sprinkle its juices over the top of the ramen and wait for it to soften."

The comedian pulled his knife free and sliced the snake into chunks, while the blind man speared the chunks with a sharpened stick, his hands moving with a surety that made the comedian question if the man could see or not. When the snake chunks were spitted, he set the stick over the fire, and the flames and smoke set about purifying the meat.

"While we wait, I would offer you a gift."

Suspicion warred within the comedian's chest. Over the years, he had met many strange people in his travels, people who had cracked. His brain told him the blind man was one of these people, broken and sad, most likely dangerous. *How pathetic. Broken people disgusted him. Just get better already.* But his heart told him to stay awhile, enjoy the man's company.

"What gift would that be?"

"In the past, I was a seer, a psychic."

"With the crystal ball and everything?"

The man shook in a silent chuckle. "It is as you say, though the crystal ball was entirely for show. For those who came to know me, all I needed was a flame, a fire, and I could tell the future."

The comedian rolled his eyes. The wasteland was filled with many strange things, but psychic powers were not one of them. He began to believe that maybe being a comedian wasn't the most worthless thing in the world. He might be a smidge above a blind psychic in the grand scheme of things.

"I sense your doubt. I can hear you when you roll your eyes."

"Uh. I wasn't."

"It's ok. It was not unexpected. I am a psychic after all."

The blind man pulled the stick from the fire and set about squeezing the snake chunks over the ramen. Small spots of grease and cooked blood dotted its surface, certainly not enough to turn the ramen from dried, crunchy noodles into soft, scrumptious ones, but it was better than nothing.

Continuing, the blind man said, "I ask that you let me fulfill my destiny."

"What destiny is that?"

"What good is a fortune teller with no fortune to tell but his own?"

64

As a comedian, he understood completely. If there were no people, the comedian would just be a man, living out his days on earth, fearing the day he would die and telling jokes to the air.

"You want to tell my fortune?"

"I thought you'd never ask."

This guy is going to kill you and wear your face skin as underwear, Oddrey said.

"Don't listen to the doll," the man said.

The comedian's jaw dropped open. "You can hear Odd?"

"No, I am deaf, but you can hear her. Will you let me tell your fortune?"

The comedian nodded.

"Then listen to my tale, my friend, for it is the tale of yourself, the tale of the world." Without warning, the blind man threw a handful of sandy soil on the fire, dousing it immediately. The cabin transformed into a funhouse of shadows, and the smoke from the fire hung between them, mixing with the smell of roasting desert snake.

The blind man's eyes rolled into the back of his head, and his jaw fell open, exposing an impossibly large mouth. Even though his massive maw didn't move, a voice emanated from deep within the man's chest.

"The east is death. The Swedish cannot be trusted. The lone rock breaks. Those that would kill will save. Time will wrap around you like a cocoon, and in this shell, you will change and heal and emerge not as a butterfly, but as a moth, its wings tattooed with the image of death's head. This is the future. A thousand, million choices led you here, but the road away contains but a few branches as the river of your life flows to your destiny. Will you take them all with you, or will you make the sacrifice when the time comes? This is the choice of your life."

With a small harrumph, the comedian said, "I choose to take everyone with me."

65

The blind man's eyes rolled back down, brown, unseeing. His gaping jaw closed, and he asked, "What did I say?"

"I can't remember it all."

"What do you mean you can't remember it all?"

"Well, if I knew there was going to be a test, I would have taken some fucking notes."

"I offer you this gift, and you spit on it."

"Oh, come on, don't be like that, blind guy."

"My name is not blind guy."

"Sheesh, if I knew you were going to be like this, I would have said 'no' to the whole fortune telling thing."

"Is everything a joke to you?"

"What are you? My wife?"

The blind man sniffed. "The snake is ready. Eat and get out."

"What about that ramen?"

"What ramen?"

When the comedian looked again, the ramen had disappeared.

"Where'd it go?"

"I put it away an hour ago, when I learned you were an ungrateful cuss of a man."

This was the way the world went in the wasteland. One minute, you'd be sitting there, pretending you were civil and still capable of holding a conversation, and the next, you'd be ready to stab a man in the heart over some ramen. If he wasn't blind, which he still had his doubts about, the comedian would have executed the man right there for crimes against humanity—namely the comedian. But the shaman had shown him kindness, even read his fortune. Something about a river? Rocks?

With greedy hands, the blind man pulled the sizzling skewer of snake chunks off the spit. The comedian offered his knife to the man, handle first. "Here take my knife. You'll burn your fingers."

With the surety and confidence of someone with sight, the blind man nodded and reached out for the blade. His fingers wrapped around the handle, and the ramen shaman speared a chunk of snake meat off the stick with the point of Rib-Tickler.

His bearded cheeks puffing out, the seer blew on the meat to cool it. As he did, a thought dawned on the comedian, and a moment of panic washed over him.

"Wait!" he called, but it was too late. The man popped the chunk of snake flesh in his mouth, his yellow teeth scraping across the blade.

The blind man chewed the snake, chomping on it, the sounds of flesh mauled by teeth filling the air between them. "'It's hot," he managed to say between chomps, sucking in air to help cool the meat. The blind man's eyes grew wide, and he spit the meat out upon the sandy soil.

"Poison!" the man shouted, pointing his finger in accusation at the comedian.

"I forgot to clean the blade," he said, knowing it was a poor apology.

He watched as the seer clutched at his throat with his hands, the desert snake's venom working its way into the blind man's body. Choking sounds filled the hut, and the comedian waited, his soul boiling in his own guilt. As the fortune teller rolled on the ground, fighting to force air past his swollen throat and into his lungs, the comedian picked up his blade and studied it.

Rib-Tickler, had been his favored sidearm for years. The metal was tarnished black where you could see it. Over the years it had tickled more than ribs. It had tickled brains, hearts, lungs. These were not crimes one easily forgot, and to remind himself of this burden, he had refused to clean the blade ever since—no. Now, his blade was poison. Rather than wiping it off, he stuffed it into the sheathe, even as the blind man convulsed in the shack. He felt bad about the seer, had totally forgotten about the snake venom

67

on his blade, but there was nothing he could do about it now.

When the blind man stopped moving, his eyes bugged out beyond belief, the comedian stood and said, "I'm sorry."

Without even taking a bite of the snake meat, he turned and fled from the small shack, knowing only that he wanted to escape, to get away from the scene of his latest crime. It was not a new experience for him.

He stepped out into the desert air, noting the sun was only a little way past where it had been when he had entered the shack. It seemed the man had been crazy, and time had marched on at a normal pace. This only made him feel the teensiest bit better, and though he wanted to run away from the cabin as fast as possible, he forced himself to walk at a leisurely pace through the small path that led between the two rounded hills.

With his head down, he walked, trying to recall the poor fortune teller's words. It was the least he could do.

If he was so good at telling fortunes, why didn't he know about the knife? Oddrey asked.

"Shut up, Odd."

The comedian stumbled into the desert hills, another taken life weighing him down.

****

The sun blasted him like a furnace, and he knew he would be cooked alive before he ever met the end of the rocky hills.

Faces cycled through his head, faces of the dead. *How many have I seen now? A hundred? A thousand?*

Each face hit him with the force of a child's punch, not painful on its own, but a thousand of them could add up over time. He turned his head from side to side, as if by doing so, he could avoid seeing the haunted conjurings of his mind.

Too dehydrated to cry, he stumbled on as the hills rose and fell around him. Time flowed like the hills, and his head began to ache. His lips, dry as the rocky soil underneath his boots, split as the wind sucked the moisture from them.

Loose rocks, treacherous as a poisoned blade, shifted underneath his feet, and the waste fog closed in on him, thick and trapped between the hills so he could only see a few feet in front of him. Panic rose within his chest, battling fear for the chance to make his heart seize and end his suffering once and for all.

Within the fog, he could see the faces of the dead, swirling in the charred mists. And then he saw the face of her.

"No!" he shouted in defiance.

He broke into a run, turning to the side to escape the beautiful, accusing face.

His legs, thick and muscular, pumped as he scrambled up the side of a large hill, gashing his fingers against the rocks and bruising his knees whenever he fell. He dared not look behind for fear of seeing the face once more.

Then the voices came, mocking and cruel.

"You left me!" a hollow voice lilted from the depths of the fog. He turned away from the voice, changing directions as if he could avoid it, and then he was lost, turning and fleeing each of his accusers.

"You killed me!"

Turn.

"You could have wiped the blade!"

Turn.

"It was just a can of Beefaroni! And what's with the stick in the butt?"

Turn, slight giggle.

"You said you loved us!"

This last brought him to a stop, and a gritty wind filled with abrasive dust and burnt life swept over him as he fell to his knees.

"Loved us!" the wind seemed to howl.

He pushed himself to his feet and fled through the swirling mist and the grinding wind, ignoring the words it threw at him. Behind his goggles, tears blinded his eyes.

Chapter 6: K. Fev Fever

The shifting sands spread out before her, stretching into the distance. *Don't go in the sand.* This advice came from a man who had once been a Chicken Kicker. *Sand can hide anything. If you can't see your foot when you walk, then it's best to go around.*

It was good, solid advice, but right now, Ajax knew she was about to ignore it. She could go around, but it would cost her time. The comedian, maniac that he was, had cut right through the sand without even thinking. If she took the time to go around, she might lose his trail. The wind, which had picked up over the last hour, might wipe away his footprints. Even now, all that remained in the sand to let her know this was the way he had gone were unnatural divots on the otherwise smooth surface of the dunes.

With a nod to herself, she set out across the sandy waste. The warm sand covered her boot up to her calf.

"Advice is just that... advice. It's not a rule. Advice was made to be ignored."

Each step felt heavier than the first as she slogged her way across the waste. She was fairly sure she knew where the comedian was headed, the path between two rounded hills. It was the way she would have chosen, although, she would have walked around the edge of the sandy desert if given a choice.

As the sun beat down, she tried to protect every inch of her skin. Her cloak was mostly perfect for this, but the swirling, gritty wind kept blowing back her hood. As she walked, she focused on the divots in the sand, occasionally lifting her head to see if she was any closer to her destination.

The hills seemed to recede further and further away every time she looked up, but it was just a trick of the eyes.

71

She knew she was making ground because when she looked behind her, she could see the edge of the waste further behind than it had been.

Somehow, she found she missed the gauzy mist of the waste. Not being able to see how far you had to go made it easy to not look ahead. It kept her focused on what was right in front of her, in this case, more sand and more footprints.

Halfway through the slow sands, she came to an area where the sand was disturbed in a wide swathe. Her boot kicked something buried in the sand, and she bent down to pluck a child's skull from the grit. Once she saw it was normal and human, she let it drop to the ground, where the sand began slowly covering it again, like a child reclaiming a precious toy from an adult who had asked to examine it.

The sucking sensation of the slow sand was unnerving, and she knew she would either successfully traverse the arid sea or wind up buried underneath tons of fine, gritty sand. As she walked, the wind whipped even harder, and her cloak flapped, snapping and twisting. She put her forearm up, blocking her eyes to keep the grit from blinding her. With her head down, she marched over the comedian's steps.

The wind was no ordinary wind. If she let her attention flag and listened to it, she could just make out the faint sound of voices carried on its gusts.

The eerie chorus made no sense, however. Many of the voices seemed to hint at acts of justice she had carried out in the last year.

"I needed to feed my family!"

This brought to mind a thief who had died begging, pleading for mercy, as if the people he had stolen from hadn't had a family to feed as well.

Onward.

"He was a raider! He deserved to die!" she shouted at the wind.

Another incident, in a town not too far from The Coop. A man mistakenly killed a traveling cinemist, a performer who traveled from town to town, reciting the movies he had seen when the world still turned. Though not a savory sort of person, he had been renowned, and his death was a loss for the communities around The Coop. She had paved the broken path.

"It was justice," Ajax grumbled under her breath.

More voices came, more voices shouted accusations, but Ajax felt no guilt. All the justice she had delivered was exactly that... and no stupid wind could tell her otherwise.

The wind was something she had never heard tell of. She had heard of polluted ponds that could twist one's reflection and drive a person mad. She had heard of trees who whispered insults as people walked among their trunks. But she had never heard of the wind trying to shame a person.

How can this even be? How can wind have a voice? And how does it know so much about my life?

She was pondering this question when her boot set foot onto solid earth, jarring her clear of her own thoughts. When she lifted her head and looked back the way she had come, she found she had made it across the sea with no trouble at all.

"She was just a child," the wind howled.

"In this world, there's no such thing as a child." She stepped forward, the wind pushing her sideways, shoving her in its frustration to make her feel guilt. In the distance, she spied a pathetic shack nestled at the beginning of a path.

The shack's boards rattled and creaked in the wind. With a slam and a clap, the shelter's door slammed open and then banged shut in a rhythm defined by the wind. To

Ajax, it almost sounded like some version of Morton's code, the technique communities used around The Coop to communicate to other nearby settlements. She had taken her turn at the drums after learning the code, banging on the massive skins in a specific rhythm to send messages from one settlement to the other. In her mind, she counted the slams and the bangs, decoding them as she strode across the thirsty earth. *Go. Flee.* She ignored the warning, another trick of the wind.

In the brief moments the door stood open, she marked the darkness inside the shack. Still, she had to see within, though she had already spotted the comedian's footprints leading away from the decrepit building. She stepped up to the darkened ruin, and though the wind could clearly rush through the building, when she opened the door, the distinct stench of age reached her nose. It smelled as if no one had been in the shack for decades.

She stood in the doorway, letting the muted sunlight filter into the shack. As her eyes adjusted, she was able to make out an ancient firepit. A mummified corpse lay curled up next to the cold ashes and charcoal. It lay on its side, its fingers curled into claws as if the person had died in horrible pain. Ajax couldn't tell if the skeleton belonged to a man or woman, but the corpse had clearly been there for some time. She couldn't lay the death of this man at the comedian's feet. But was it a coincidence that where he walked another body appeared?

There was nothing in the shack for her, so she turned and let the wind slam the door shut. As it did, the structure finally gave way, and the force of the door slamming into the frame sent the whole shack tumbling to the dust.

"Anything good in there?" a man asked.

Ajax turned, her hand going to her mace.

In the crotch of the two hills, a man stood, perhaps the most handsome man Ajax had ever laid eyes on.

"Stay right there," she commanded.

The man put his hands up in mock surrender. He flashed a toothy grin full of perfect white teeth. That whiteness, that ivory shine did something to her knees, and only through the gift of her training was she able to keep her feet.

The man, still flashing those pearly whites, approached, and Ajax yelled, "I'm warning you!"

"Was there anything good in there?" he repeated.

Once Ajax was able to tear her eyes away from the man's face, she noted he was dressed like a raider. His clothing was a mishmash of sporting goods, leather items, and stitched together clothing that was more stitches than cloth. On his hip, he wore a machete in a hard plastic holster. The bare ends of his fingers twitched, and yet, still he smiled at her.

"Stay right there," she said, though secretly, she wanted him to come closer.

"I'm no danger," the man said.

"I know that. It's just... I'm following someone, and I don't want you to mess up their tracks."

"Ooh. Following someone. Are you a detective?"

"How many of you are there?"

The man spread his arms wide as if to show he had nothing up his sleeve, and he asked, "Do you see anyone else?"

"You're a raider, right?"

"Aren't we all?"

"I'm not."

The man's smile faded, and he looked at the mace in her hand. He winked at her, but she could tell he was on guard now.

"Why are you looking for him?"

"How do you know it's a him?"

"Because I saw him run from that shack."

"How long ago?"

The raider looked around, scanning the sky as if the answer was written in the clouds. "Oh, who's to say? Time's kinda funny out here."

Ajax could feel the sands slipping through the hourglass, and she wished she had one, anything to help hold time in place. The raider—the handsome raider—was right. Time was funny out here. An hourglass could hold it off, create a small pocket of order in a place that otherwise seemed intent on making absolutely no sense at all.

"Back off."

The man took one step back, and Ajax scanned the ground, locating the comedian's footprints once again.

"My name's Kevin Fever."

What a ridiculous name. Besides, if anyone's feeling feverish around here, it's me. "I didn't ask your name."

"May I ask yours?"

Still, he was fairly polite for a raider. "Name's Ajax."

"I like names with x's in them."

"I'm going now."

"Mind if I tag along?"

Ajax turned, a retort on her lips. But then she thought of the chaos. She thought of the shifting sands, the winds that knew her past, the tumbling shacks, and the evercracks, and she thought maybe this man, this Kevin Fever, could offer some sort of defense against the chaotic nature of the wastes. Where two humans walked, they brought order. This was the truth, and this was one of the reasons Chicken Kickers didn't go out on their own. "You may follow along."

The man grinned, and though she didn't mean to, she snuck a look at the bulge in the crotch of his leather pants. *Maybe this is a bad idea. He could have anything stuffed in there.*

"Just keep where I can see you," Ajax said.

76

"Same to you," the man replied with the barest hint of a wink.

Was that flirting? No. Definitely not.

"Keep off the tracks," she said, pointing at the ground with her mace.

"You got it."

Together the two began their walk. To Ajax's surprise, the path did not lead between the two, firm, rounded hills. It started out that way, then a short while on, it veered sharply to the left, over the hill, so up the hill they went, Kevin Fever walking ahead of her, his hips swaying from side to side in his leather pants.

God, I've been out here too long.

****

"Looks like he's running," Kevin said.

Ajax nodded. The comedian's tracks did seem frantic, hurried.

The studiousness with which the raider studied the tracks was encouraging, but maybe he was just laying a trap for her, proving himself handy in order to trick her into letting down her guard. Then he would spring, and pin her to the ground and…

Around them, the wind had settled, allowing the mists to move in like chokemoss. How there could be more mist after all that wind was a mystery, but such was the wasteland.

"What'd this guy do to you?"

"Nothing."

"Do you want him to do something to you?" he asked, looking over his shoulder with an impish grin on his face.

She wanted to hate it, wanted to see something dangerous in that grin. But that's not what she saw. *I see nothing.*

77

"He's a murderer."

The grin disappeared from his face.

"He kill someone you love?"

Ajax shook her head.

"Kill someone that someone you love loved?

Ajax shook her head.

"In that case, it's best to just leave well enough alone."

"Too many people leave well enough alone. And then they leave not well enough alone. And then they leave bad alone. And then we're in the mess we're in right now."

"That's one way of looking at it."

"It's the only way of looking at it."

K. Fev, as she had begun calling him in her mind, shrugged, and they walked for some time in absolute silence. Their boots crunched over the rocky soil, but other than that, the silence was total and complete. Though for some odd reason, Ajax could hear her heart beating in her ears. It was actually quite pleasant, and then K. Fev opened his beautiful mouth again.

"This guy got any food on him? Any water?"

"I don't know."

"What do you know?"

Ajax sighed. She was about to tell the man to go on his way. His presence, though it helped stave off chaos, was not worth all this conversation. But then they came upon a spot where the tracks changed.

"Looks like he collapsed," K. Fev said. "See here?" He pointed out the obvious signs, things Ajax already knew, and somehow, this infuriated her. "Maybe he's tiring out. How long have you been tracking this guy?"

"Don't know. Like you said, time's kinda funny out here."

K. Fev scanned the sky. It had darkened somewhat and evening was coming on. Already she could see the faint green of the night sky.

"Well, we're not going to catch him tonight."

Ajax nodded her head.

"Shall we make camp?"

Ajax shrugged. She had hoped to make camp or part ways with Kevin Fever before the onset of evening. At least then she would have been able to sleep, as deeply as one could sleep in the wastes, but still it was better than the negligible amount of slumber she was in line for that evening.

The wind howled as they made their camp on the ground. There was no fuel for a fire, and the night turned chill quickly, so they laid on the ground, pulling their clothes tight about their faces. The wind faded once more, and above the burnt mists, Ajax studied the glowing sky and the handful of stars strong enough to show through the shifting green light. The constellations of her youth came back to her. *There's Iron Man, each star of the constellation marking one of his famed blue-white repulsors. Over there, Hawkeye with his shining belt and his bow and arrow. Thor's hammer, Mjolnir, and there, little Mjolnir.*

With her hand on the haft of her mace, and her eyes hidden by the cowl of her cloak, she listened for the tell-tale sound of shifting sand underneath a body. If Kevin Fever came for her, she would be ready... although, maybe she wanted him to come for her? *Where did that thought come from?*

She grunted, telling herself not to be one of those weak-willed women who fell for a pretty face. It was the pretty ones you had to watch out for. And, for all she knew, he was a raider. Laying with a raider would be against the code. No sleeping with the enemy, not out in the wastes.

But she'd never seen a raider quite as handsome as K. Fev. He didn't have the typical hallmarks of a raider. His eyes weren't dead. When he smiled, it seemed like he actually felt it. It wasn't some wolfish grin that made Ajax feel like the man was mentally marking the best cuts of her body to eat later. His face was free of the scarring and pockmarking present on so many raiders' faces. You didn't become a raider because you were smart, and sooner or later, all raiders wound up disfigured in some way—if not physically, then spiritually. And that's what was giving Ajax such trouble. As far as she could tell, K. Fev was perfect in every way.

Without thinking twice, he had joined in her quest to find the comedian. The beautiful hunk of man didn't even care why she was looking for him. And yet, she couldn't shake the feeling of being led astray.

No one was that nice. Not anymore. Or maybe she was changed—"jaded" the old timers called it. Maybe she couldn't look at a normal person with perfectly normal intentions and handsome pillowy lips without thinking, *How is this person going to try and screw me over?*

It happened often enough. Ajax had met many people on the road. The handsome ones were the dangerous ones. Not that all the scarred, pus-oozing unfortunates out there were angels, but at least they provided an outward sign one should be on guard. With Kevin Fever, there was nothing.

"You awake?" a medium-pitched voice asked. She could listen to that voice for hours if she knew it wasn't going to laugh over her dead body at some point.

Ajax was tempted to keep quiet, pretend she slumbered, but she wanted to hear his voice some more, hear what interesting things he had to say, and she wasn't going to sleep that night anyway. *So why the hell not?*

"Yeah."

"It's weird to sleep out here, right? Underneath all that green."

"Yeah." Each time she spoke, it seemed her vocabulary was pared away until all she was left with were single syllable answers. Try as she might to channel the pithy, cavalier romanticism of a superhero, she was not built that way.

She heard K. Fev shift in the sand, some five-feet away from her, and when she turned to look at him, he was leaning his head on the palm of his hand, his supporting elbow sunk into the sand.

In the green light of the radglow, she could just make out the shine of his eyes. He was awake and watching her.

"Where do you come from?" Kevin Fever asked.

This question put her back on guard, and she didn't answer for some time. Finally, she hit him with a question of her own. "Why do you ask?"

"I just wanted to know if there are more people like you out there. Is there a place filled with Ajaxes?"

"What would you do if there were?"

"Why, I'd want to see it. Sounds like heaven to me."

Ugh. It was a bad flirt, but it wasn't like she was a great romantic or anything, and so she let it go. Instead, she countered with, "For all I know, you could be a raider."

"We're all raiders at one point or another."

"Not me."

A snickering laugh echoed in the dark. "Come on. You wouldn't have made it this far if you hadn't killed anyone."

"Never said I didn't kill anyone. Just said I wasn't a raider."

Kevin Fever fell silent, and when next he spoke, she noticed there was less amusement in his voice. "Well, what makes you different from a raider? Raiders kill. You kill. What's the difference?"

The answer was not difficult for Ajax, but tempering her response and keeping it civil was. "What do you mean 'What's the difference?' There's a huge difference between why I kill someone and why a raider kills someone."

"I don't see it."

"Well, for one, I kill people for good, for order."

"Who is order?"

"Order's not a person. It's an ideal."

"Oh, order. Like, I'd like to order a double cheeseburger. Got it."

Ajax sputtered in the green night. "No, that's not it at all. Order, as in putting the world right and maintaining the way things are supposed to be."

"Wait... you kill people 'for the way things ought to be?' That's worse than a raider."

Ajax's jaw clenched. "How so?"

"Well, a raider kills because they're hungry, and they have no other way to survive. But to kill for an idea, something that's made up in your head, well, that's absolutely ridiculous. Killing to survive is ok. Man's been doing it for years. Why, I bet you've killed an animal or two to feed yourself. How is that any different than killing a human?"

"They're animals."

"But they're alive. They think and feel, not in ways we can recognize, but they do. Do you agree?"

"I guess so."

"You know so. Now, if I kill a living, thinking animal that's a part of nature, is that not against this order of yours?"

"Who are you?"

"I'm Kevin fucking Fever, and don't you forget it." He smiled in the green light, and the way he said the line made her feel like it was a personal catchphrase, something he uttered whenever given the chance. "Now answer the question. Is it, or is it not, against order for you to kill an animal?" he continued.

"It's not. It's the natural way of things."

"But could you not just grow plants and eat those? Do you have to mash up a squirrel with that shiny little mace there?"

Ajax was fully awake now. All thoughts of sleep had fled from her head. Kevin Fever was asking a lot of interesting questions, but she was mostly annoyed by them. All that mattered to her now was showing K. Fev how wrong he was about order. "There is an order in nature, and we're at the top of it. If I choose to eat a squirrel, then I have that right, and there's nothing wrong with it."

K. Fev mumbled his assent. "Uh-huh. Uh-huh. But what if I were to tell you that in the natural order of things, the members of humanity have an order as well."

"No person is greater than another."

"Bah!" Kevin Fever spat, barely able to stifle his laughter. "Even you don't believe that!" With that, K. Fev sat up and pulled his shirt off exposing an abdomen which would put several Avengers to shame. "Look at this," he said, slapping his taught abs. "They used to call me Mini-Wheats because I was so shredded."

Though she liked what she saw, she wasn't ready to concede the argument. "Looks mean nothing. And what are Mini-Wheats?"

"Dunno. Just a line I heard a rai—raven say one day." He waved his hand in the air, attempting to cover the slip-up, but Ajax had marked it well. "But you have to admit I, myself, and you, are worth more than a leper or a rad-rotter. They're still human, but they're not worth as much as us. If one of them has something we want, it's only natural we take it from them in whatever manner we choose to see fit."

"It is not order to steal from the weak and helpless. It is chaos."

"I disagree. While it might be morally reprehensible, and I can agree with you on that point, it is order for the stronger to take from the weaker. Protecting

83

the weak—now that's chaos. Allowing the suffering and the sick to roam among the healthy, well that's just all sorts of chaos waiting to happen."

Ajax didn't know what to do. She had never been much of a philosopher back at The Coop. She grasped the principles of order, knew what to do to protect it, but as far as the underlying principles behind those beliefs were concerned, it was just the way it was. She had never questioned them or thought to break them down and analyze the tenets of order.

"Shut up," Ajax said.

K. Fev smiled at her, his white teeth shining green in the glow, and she didn't know whether she wanted to bash his teeth in or kiss him. She lay back on the ground and pulled the hood of her cloak tight around her face. A few minutes later, she heard the sounds of K. Fev shifting, and soon a soft snoring came from his direction. Though she tried to sleep, her mind filled with all sorts of thoughts, some about order, some about chaos, some about... other things.

Chapter 7: In a Basement, In the Past

The comedian stumbled through the wastes, putting space between himself and his pursuers, unbeknownst to him. With thoughts of the past slicing through his brain, he pushed onward as if he could escape the haunted whispers by simply continuing to move.

But isn't that what you've always been doing?

"Stow it, Odd."

The wasteland had stretched onward, rocky, desolate, inhospitable. His water and food were completely depleted, and he stood in the wastes with his back, legs, and feet aching. It was only a matter of time now. Death, the biggest joke of all, came for him. At the beginning of every person's life, Death said, "Here, take all this time. Take these emotions, these feelings. Discover the thrills of joy and love." Then, just when you thought you understood everything about the world and how it worked, and you were ready to make a perfect life for yourself, only then did Death come along and pull the rug out from underneath you, snatching it all away. It all goes away.

"Haha. Good one Death."

Maybe you just need to stop.

"No."

Maybe you just need to think, face the past.

"Nope. Gotta keep moving." Though his head swam and his body had stopped sweating some time in the middle of the night, the comedian pressed forward, stumbling up the side of a large hill dotted with scrub grasses. "You'll see. Top of this rise, it'll be a whole new world. No more rocks. No more waste grass. No more stinky mist. You'll see."

Maybe you should just think about them. Maybe you could talk to them.

"They're dead, Odd. Talking to the dead is a waste of time."

You're dead. Should I stop talking to you?

The comedian stumbled, gashing his knee on a sharp stone. He could feel the cloth of his pants sticking to his knee. "I'm not dead, Odd. I'm still kickin'. Does a dead man bleed?" Though it was like lifting a boulder, he pushed himself off the ground and continued his ascent.

You're pretending to be alive.

"Psshh. You should talk. You're a freaking doll head. Raggedy Oddrey."

Very mature.

"I know."

The comedian stumbled again, and then he fell on the slopes of a hill. The crest of the rise was only a few feet ahead, but to make it, he was going to have to crawl. He didn't have the energy to walk upright.

Just stop.

For the first time in a while, he actually listened to Oddrey's advice. He let himself sag onto the rocky slope, his bearded cheek pressed against jagged rocks. His chest rose and fell as his body slid back into a less thumping, blood-roaring existence. When the pain of the rocks became too great on his cheeks, he rolled onto his back and stared up at the green night sky. For the first time in forever, he let himself remember... he let himself live.

****

It was funny, kind of. He always thought the end of the world would be a little more telegraphed. Like, one day while out at the store, there would be an announcement on the radio, some sort of dire message interrupting the natural flow of events. Everyone would stop and listen as some voice with heavy doses of gravitas and a fatherly timbre calmly announced the end of the world.

86

Somewhere, in someplace, this message has been prepared. It sat typed on a white sheet of paper with the seal of the United States of America upon it. This paper sat in a file, which sat in a file cabinet, which sat in an office. When the time was needed, someone important, but generally unknown, would call an office aide, and send them running down to the office with a key to pull out that single sheet of paper. The office aide would run the paper over to a man whose sole job was to sit at a desk and wait for the end of the world. That's the way it had to be. You never knew when the end of the world was going to happen. You couldn't have that guy having another job or something. How would it look if some random asteroid, knocked out of its orbit by a Jupiter fart, came out of nowhere and there was no one there to read the end of the world statement because they were out doing voiceover work for the trailer of *Breakin' 3: The Boogie Tree* to make ends meet? That would be a disaster in and of itself.

Instead, the office aide would hand the sheet of paper to this bored bastard sitting in front of a microphone for a 12-hour shift. He'd be incredibly smart because all he did was read for twelve hours. He could tell you everything about the complications of fracking. He's read every book about pug dogs that was ever published, because he liked pugs for some reason. If he were transported back in time, he could actually recreate electricity, thus making him a god. But none of that mattered now because it was time to read the statement, and he did. "Blah, blah, blah, end of the world. Hold each other. Have a pray, etc. etc."

And then everyone in that grocery store, listening to that crackling speaker, that god-like intercom, and that dulcet-voiced angel, would share a look. One old lady would fall to her knees, her hands clasped in front of her chin, and a big man in a flannel shirt and a Gone Fishin' hat, someone who you wouldn't think had a heart, would kneel next to her and pray as well while resting a

87

comforting hand on her shoulder. Then, everyone would calmly finish their purchases and head home for one last night with their loved ones.

At least, that's the way he thought it was going to be, but it wasn't like that at all. The end of the world was much worse.

It wasn't a single bomb or asteroid. No velvety-voiced radio man ever cut in at the grocery store. The end of the world was not one devastating blow. It was more like a death by a thousand cuts. Of course, everything could be laid at the feet of humanity. It's like humanity said to the entire world, "You know—we're going out, but before we do, we're gonna take all you other motherfuckers with us." In this case "motherfuckers" were other species, plants, whole environments, and general decency.

Cut one: a warming, out-of-whack, environment.

Cut two: an energy shortage.

Cut three: supply chain issues.

Cut four: rampant sickness.

Cut five: America's Got Talent.

And so on and so forth. Each cut compounded the others and the blood of the world leached out onto the dry, dusty soil. And then the Earth turned into a corpse. Its body started to dry out and rot. The evercracks came. Then came the sickness. Then came the creatures. Then came the bombs, followed by newer more virile creatures and sicknesses.

It wasn't until the comedian's neighbor Hugh died that the comedian realized that, yes, the world was in fact dying. For weeks, he had watched the TV, watching as humanity fought back against the thousand plagues of the world, making small but meaningful headway in the battle against species extinction. Then one day, the updates just stopped, and Hugh's daughter Phoebe ate Hugh—dragged his guts right out onto the brown, dusty lawn and ate his colon bite by bite.

The TV cut out, the radio cut out, and the Internet went away, and the only sign they had of civilization after that came in the form of smoke signals... the smoke of buildings burning in the distance—the smoke of bombs as they traveled across the sky on the way to their destinations. No one knew why they were launched or what was meant to be accomplished by them. They were just there one day, streaking across the sky, tracing lines in the atmosphere, and that was the worst part, not knowing why the world came to an end. Not having an answer, not having someone to blame it on. People need a villain... but sometimes, shit just happens. That sentiment would become the motto of the wasteland. Shit happens.

He was sitting out back drinking a mix of Country Time Lemonade and whiskey he had found in Hugh's house when he saw the bombs racing overhead. It only took him a moment to drain the rest of his drink, and then he was inside, grabbing Audrey and his wife and dragging them down into the basement.

"Where are we going, Daddy?"

"Don't worry about it."

In the basement, they huddled in silence. The dim basement lights were never quite bright enough to chase away the shadows of the basement and their minds. Though they didn't hear the bombs fall, they felt their impact in the ground. Not all at the same time, but one after another. Different times and distances led to a staggered impact for the bombs, and dust drifted down from the floorboards above. The house around them creaked its complaint, and the earth itself seemed to moan.

"What is it?" Audrey asked.

"It's nothing, baby."

But it was something. It was the end. It was the end of everything, only he didn't know it yet. Sometime that evening, he crept up to the kitchen and pulled their food down into the basement. In the street, he saw Phoebe eating

Hugh's foot. The poor girl had been munching on that body for days now.

Then they hid, pulling into their shells like disturbed turtles. They thought to wait it out… thought to make the best of their time, stay in the basement as long as they could. They sang songs, told stories, tried to pretend like this was just a blip in the world, and everything would return to normal in no time at all. Why, in just a few short months, Audrey would be going off to middle school, ready to start the 6th grade with whoever was leftover.

The lights went out with the bombs, so it was a dark time. When Audrey had to use the restroom, she had to go in a bucket illuminated with a small pool of light from her flashlight. It hurt him to see his daughter squint at the light.

When their food ran out, his small family emerged as cave people, shrinking and covering their eyes to protect from the glaring orange sky. Overhead, clouds blocked out everything, and the grass lay dead and crispy beneath their feet while the stench of the burned world stung their noses.

With their stomachs growling, they crept through their neighborhood, looking for signs of life. Phoebe was gone, and so was Hugh. It was a new world they were born into, and they were as helpless as proverbial babes. His wife, Raina, looked nothing like his wife. That woman had been an energetic beauty with a soft face and a kind heart. This woman was like the dead grass that crunched underneath their feet, hard and cold.

Raina had always been a family woman. She came from a large family, more of a tribe really, and now they were all dead as far as they knew. They had moved from California to Montana when Audrey was born to give her the smalltown life Raina valued. When Raina herself was a child, she had grown up on a ranch in Utah with a dozen siblings and cousins running wild in the countryside of their family manor.

It didn't take him long to figure out there was something wrong with his wife. Even when they found food, she ate half-heartedly. Her conversations consisted of one-word answers, and she would be content to sleep all day if he let her. He understood depression, the mechanics of it, the realities of it, but he was no doctor, hadn't been much of anything really, just a hard-working guy who dabbled in a little bit of everything. What did he know about the mind? What did he know about the depths of Raina's depression? They toiled on, and he thought she would snap out of it eventually. Back then, he still had hope.

They lived this way, like the occasional zombie they saw walking in the woods, doing nothing but eating and groaning. Weeks passed by as the sky swirled and the weather turned cold and miserable, the sun blotted out by all the crap in the air. They kept inside for the most part, avoiding the radiation they were sure was in the atmosphere. The people had vanished, disappeared, taken their vehicles and set out for other places. Where did they go? Or were they hiding? It would be a long, lonely time until they saw people. During that time, Raina devolved, turned into nothing more than a shambling, grunting animal. Audrey didn't understand.

"Does Mommy hate us?" she asked one night while Raina snored for the tenth hour in a row.

"She's just going through something, baby."

"Will she be alright?"

"Oh, yeah," he lied. "You'll see. A couple more days, and she'll be good as new." Audrey accepted this without question, and he felt like a shit for lying to her. But what good would it do to say, "I think she's lost"?

A month after that, shivering and with his ribs showing through his shirt, a caravan of people in trucks had come through their town, firing off guns, wasting ammunition that would be worth a fortune in but a year's

91

time. Wasteful—but these people didn't care. They traveled in armored trucks, men and women and even a few children, living life like it was gonna be over for them tomorrow, and who was to say it wasn't?

He heard the gunfire before he ever heard the trucks, and then he was dragging his wife and daughter into the basement of a building.

"No," Raina said, breaking free of his grip.

"What do you mean no?" he hissed, careful not to speak too loudly, lest they invite the attention of the scavenging caravan.

"I'm not going to hide anymore."

"They could be crazies. They could be murderers."

"Or they could be people just like us."

Audrey sat watching this exchange, chewing on her lower lip.

"They could be rapists," he hissed, quiet enough to prevent Audrey from overhearing.

"So?"

And for the first time in his life, he realized he didn't actually know his wife at all, not anymore. She shrugged her shoulders at him and ripped her hand away. "I'm going."

He laughed then, as if she were telling a joke. "You're not serious."

"I don't want to live like this, like cockroaches scurrying from one hiding place to the next. I don't want that for Audrey. What sort of life is this for her? She should be around people, other children, not hiding and worrying every time there's a noise." She turned then and walked away from him.

Audrey looked to him for guidance, her eyes round and large.

"She's coming back, right Daddy?"

But he didn't have an answer.

"Daddy?"

Instead of answering, of calming her down, he dragged Audrey into the nearest house, and then into the basement, closed the door behind them and then stacked whatever basement junk he could find against the door.

In the darkness, they huddled together, his arms wrapped around her in an attempt to provide her with some sense of security, false though it may be. But a false sense was better than no sense.

The basement hung heavy and black around them, unlit by even those useless rectangular windows you'd sometimes find in basements. They were down to four senses in that blackness.

He felt the warm tears of his daughter on his forearm as she sat between his legs with his arm around her neck. The rot of something decomposing in the corner assaulted his nose. He tasted his own fear in the back of his throat, and in the dim recesses of his mind, he heard the screams of his wife as the caravan discovered her.

Were the screams imagined or real? He wanted to ask Audrey, but then thought better of it. *Why did she leave? Am I really that bad, that worthless?*

His daughter sniffled in the darkness, and he felt her entire body trembling.

"Hey, Aud."

"What?" she managed to groan.

"What do you call a fish wearing a bowtie?"

She didn't answer, so he went ahead and delivered the punchline anyway. "Sofishticated."

She didn't laugh. Who could at that time? But for a moment, one pure moment, she was able to forget about the fact her mother had abandoned her, and that was good enough for him. He rattled off joke after joke, each worse than the next one.

The screaming above seemed to grow louder, although in the basement he couldn't be entirely sure he was hearing anything at all.

93

"Shh," he whispered as the sound of boots on the floorboards above echoed throughout the darkness.

The screaming stopped, and he heard voices at the top of the stairs. The rattle of the handle. The sharp intake of Audrey's breath. He squeezed his eyes shut. The sound of an axe chopping down wood. Chop. Chop. Chop.

"Hey, Aud. How do you get a squirrel to like you?"

Chop.

"Act like a nut."

Chop.

Voices.

When he saw the first rays of light, he squeezed Aud tighter, pulled her to his chest.

Then they started throwing the items of his pitiful barricade down the stairs, and he knew they were coming down.

Voices filtered down, people voices, ordinary, plain. In the background, more screaming. Raina.

The first words he could make out were... *Welcome to Beandick Arnold's.*

Chapter 8: Beandick Arnold's

Beandick Arnold's? That's not what they said. He opened his eyes and found himself face to face with an Asian man sporting a large, bushy beard.

Ordinarily, if the comedian was confronted with a stranger's face inches from his own, his first reaction would be to pull his knife free and wave it around in the man's guts. But he was too exhausted for that at the moment.

"What the fuck is Beandick Arnold's?"

"Why, it's ma farm."

With that nonsensical answer sorted out, he closed his eyes and went back to sleep.

****

Sometime later, he awoke in a dream. At least, he thought it was a dream. How else could he explain the lush green foliage surrounding him. He sat up and marveled at row after row of green plant tops jutting from a rich brown earth. All around, rock and stone hills rose, creating a shallow depression where every inch was covered by lush greenery.

As he stood up, something dropped to the ground. At his feet, he spotted an old plastic canteen. Licking his dry lips, he picked it up off the ground, unscrewed the top, and gave it a deep sniff. Water, rich with minerals. On the odd chance this was all a dream and he would wake up at any moment, he tilted the canteen up to his lips, gulping the water down. When the water stopped coming out, he lay back down and held the canteen upside down, waiting for the last few drops of water to tumble free and onto his tongue.

He was doing this with his eyes closed when he felt a shadow fall over him, blocking out the weak glare of the sun. He opened his eyes to find the man from before standing over him.

"Is this a dream?" the comedian asked.

"What is a dream?" the man asked.

"You don't know? Or is this some sort of philosophical question?"

"You tell me."

The comedian studied the man. With a freshly hydrated brain, by his standards anyway, he found he liked this man. He didn't know why. He hated most people, would rather leave them dead and rotting in a gutter than be forced to actually talk to them, but there was something about this man that felt... magic. It was a stupid thought. He was just a man like any other. Probably wanted him to do something sexual in exchange for the water he had drunk.

The comedian pushed himself to his feet and handed the canteen to the man. "Thanks for the water." It was then he noticed his gear was missing. "Now where's my stuff?"

The man didn't speak, just lifted an arm and pointed in the general direction of an old canvas tent. The comedian strode over and found all his gear piled within. Feeling naked, he put everything in the right place, backpack, sword, jacket. With his back turned to the mysterious man, he checked to see if anything was missing. It wasn't, which was good because it meant he didn't have to kill the man who gave him water.

You sure? Odd asked.

"Sure about what?"

The killing.

"I'm never sure."

He stood with a groan, already thirsting for more water. Though his body was sore and his soul tortured, he decided to press on. His cheeks creaking like old leather, he

96

plastered a winning smile on his face. And then he turned, ready to put on the show.

"Quite a place you have here."

The man smiled at him, a good-natured smile, free of artifice; it made the comedian feel strange.

When's the last time I've seen such a smile? He couldn't remember.

"It's nice. I like it," the man said. When he smiled, he presented teeth that were only a little gray with age.

"You here all by yourself?"

"Plants keep me company. Come, you must be hungry. It's been a spell since I had any company. Hain't seen my friend the shack man in a bit."

At this, a wave of guilt washed over the comedian. Beandick turned, and the comedian followed him over to a row of stalls, piled high with fruits and vegetables. The produce was unlike anything he had ever seen before.

With a trembling hand, the funnyman reached out and grabbed a fist-sized fruit with bright red skin. It was firm. "What is this?" he asked.

"That right there is a pomato, half-potato, half-tomato. Puree it up, and it makes a delicious soup."

"Did you make this?"

"I don't right reckon how the soil 'round here works. I plant one thing and sump'n else comes up. It's been quite an adventure discovering what the soil gives."

The comedian spotted another fruit, or vegetable, or something. As large as a volleyball and covered in green leathery skin, it was striped like a watermelon. "Is that a watermelon?"

"Nope. I calls it a dirtermelon. Got the flesh of a watermelon, but tastes like beets. Still, it's good in a pinch if'n you're hungry."

The comedian ambled down the stalls, picking up strange fruit after strange fruit, marveling at the unique little treasures. When his mouth began to water, he turned to Beandick and said, "How much?"

Beandick plucked the straw hat from his head and scratched his scalp through his thinning black hair. "Well, nothin's free these days, so I guess I gotta charge you something." A piece of straw switched from side to side in his mouth, the end bobbing up and down as he contemplated his fee. "I notice you got yourself a little pianer there. I could might use a song or two to pass the time. I suppose if'n you can rustle me up a tune or two, I might see fit to provide you with a full belly."

"It's a deal." The comedian felt fortunate, as if someone in the wasteland was looking out for him. It had been a while since he'd felt this way, and his mind brimmed with possibilities.

"Well, grab what you want, and we'll have ourselves a little pick-a-nick."

The comedian looked at the strange fruits, selected a few, and together, they sat on the ground, on the rich brown earth. He unlimbered the Fetus Grand from his back, set it softly upon the soil, and then cracked his knuckles to get them nice and loose. He plinked on the keys for a few seconds with an apologetic smile in Beandick's direction. "It's been a while," he said by way of apology.

The farmer nodded, leaning back on his elbows and looking up in the sky, that piece of straw bobbing up and down in his mouth. He was in no hurry.

The comedian began to play. It was a song his daugh—a song someone he knew used to like. Simple and easy to play, it was all about the singing. He sang the song, a pop tune with a catchy simplicity. His rusted pipes garbled the words, but right there, in the middle of all that greenness, he felt as if he didn't have a care in the world, and he let his voice rise and fall. It echoed off the mountain walls of the tiny valley.

With his eyes closed, he let the song flow through him, channeling memories, painful and sweet. Behind his goggles, he trapped his tears with his eyelids, and his voice cracked a few times. When he finished the song, the last echoes of the Fetus Grand fading into nothingness, he felt better, calmer. When he opened his soggy eyes, Beandick was still there, his head tilted back and his own eyes closed.

Without opening them, Beandick said, "That was wonderful. I miss Justin Bieber... well, his music, not the man."

"No one misses the man."

With one song done, and his debt partially paid, he grabbed a pomato and took a bite from it. It tasted horrible, the flesh firm like an apple but tangy like an unripe tomato. In the middle, hundreds of dark seeds floated in a cold, purple jelly. But his throat didn't swell up, and his mouth didn't tingle, so he finished the horrid fruit-vegetable, filling his belly as it hadn't been filled in some time.

"You been out there a long time?" Beandick asked.

"As long as everyone else at this point."

"Uh-huh. That's a mighty long time then."

"What about you? How long have you lived here?"

Beandick sat up then, his eyes darting to the side as he tried to access his memories. "I don't rightly know. Seems like I been here all my life. Seems like all I remember is planting and plucking and weeding." Beandick took a moment to scan his farm. "I don't know."

At this apparent memory lapse, the comedian stopped eating, wondering if the fruit had some sort of memory-wiping property. What if eating the food from the farm made it so you never wanted to leave, you just wanted to keep eating and planting and eating and planting? In his mind, he already wanted to stay here, to live among the quiet hills, dig his hands into the dirt, and forget the outside world even existed.

Beandick finished doing some mental calculations, and then said, "Oh, it was about five years ago as far as I can tell. Ain't got no calendar out here, so it's hard to figger, but it was back when the meteor came."

Everyone remembered the meteor, purple and ominous. It had hung in the air for a month before crashing into earth, adding insult to injury. It had been cloudy for a week after that. The comedian's worries vanished, and he felt foolish for even having them, not that he showed it. He had long since buried all physical signs of embarrassment. Oh, he felt it from time to time, but no one would ever know.

Except for me.

The comedian ignored Odd's mocking words. "Did you just find it like this?"

"Well, when I started, it was just a small patch of green sitting next to a muddy spring. But the water was clean and didn't tingle, so I decided to set up shop out here. Seemed as good a place as any, and it has been."

The comedian polished off the pomato, and he picked up the next item of produce. Roundy and fuzzy like a peach, he had it halfway to his mouth before Beandick yelled, "Stop!"

The sheer panic in the man's voice halted him in mid-bite.

"That ain't a fruit! That's a spider egg."

The comedian quickly pulled the egg from his mouth, and he studied the fuzzy ball.

Beandick stood and took the egg from his hand. "Now how did that get in there?" He began to walk to the edge of the farm, and the comedian, having nothing else better to do, walked along with him.

At the edge of the greenery, the farmer stopped and lobbed the fuzzy ball up the slope of the hill. It shattered on the ground, the flesh of the faux, peach-like egg breaking open, and a swarm of dark shapes emerged, skittering over each other. A thousand spiders unfurled their bodies and ran this way and that, feeding upon each other and looking for a way to survive. Their struggle and chaos reminded him of those terrible days when he had emerged from his home in Montana, everyone fighting each other for food and resources instead of working together and trying to put the world back together.

"Thanks," he said to Beandick, cognizant he had most certainly avoided a nasty situation.

"Sorry 'bout that. I don't know why them damn things like to lay them eggs up in my stalls, but they do. It's like they're hoping to catch one of us unaware."

The comedian patted Beandick on the arm, and they returned to the spot where he'd left his gear. When he sat next to the Fetus Grand, he shrugged off the fact he had left his gear sitting unattended out in the open. Normally, he would never go more than a few feet from his stuff, and certainly never without Side-Splitter, but something about this place calmed him.

He squatted down, and Beandick sat across from him, reclining on his back and staring at the sky above.

They sat in silence, a gentle breeze flowing down the hills and into the valley. The waste mist didn't come down here, as if it respected this small patch of heaven.

Maybe this is heaven.

Heaven doesn't have fist-sized spider eggs and watermelons that taste like dirt, Odd said.

She was right. Whatever this place was, it was fool's gold. Sure, a man could eat and drink here, live out the string of their days, but the comedian had other things to do. In silence, he ate another pomato. He trusted it, had already eaten one and had nothing bad happen to him, and despite the revolting seedy middle of the fruit-vegetable, it provided him with extra moisture. As he chomped on his meal, he asked the relaxing farmer a question.

"Why do they call you Beandick Arnold?"

His hands behind his head and one-leg crossed over the other, he spoke without opening his eyes. "Used to be a trader. Used to travel around the wastes, peddling my fruits and veggies. It got so everyone around here knew me. When I'd come up on a town, they'd yell, 'The trader is coming! The trader is coming!' Well, some people heard the word traitor, you know, like one who stabs someone else in the back. One genius, he comes up one day, and he calls me Benedict Arnold, the traitor. And then, the guy next to him, he's about as bright as a moonless night, goes, 'Your name's Beandick Arnold?' From there, it just sort of stuck. Spread around the communities out here, and shit, now I don't even 'member ma real name."

The comedian nodded. It was as good an eponym as anything else he had heard in the wasteland.

"I expect you'll want to be moving on," Beandick said.

The comedian nodded.

"You know where you're headed?"

"Ike."

"Oh, Ike. I ain't been there in a squirrel's age."

"You know it?"

"I do. It's about ten miles thataway." He said this last while jabbing his thumb in a random direction.

"Anything you can tell me 'bout the place?"

"Well, it's been about seven raider cycles since I been out that way. Only thing I can really say is watch yourself when you get there. But you probably already knew to do that. Oh, and stay away from the meatballs."

The comedian nodded, filing the information away, and then packed up his belongings.

"Before you go, can I ask you a question?" Beandick asked.

"Shoot," the comedian said as he settled the Fetus Grand on his shoulders.

"What's your name?"

"Why?"

"Just wanna know the name of the man I fed, the man who can sing a song."

The comedian, his life saved by this mysterious trader, granted the man's request and then headed on his way, walking doggedly in the direction the man had indicated.

Chapter 9: A Raider's Way

When Ajax awoke, a fine layer of waste grit covered her, the small bits of ash and burnt life that floated in the atmosphere, only to rain down upon the world every now and then. She wiped at her face, wondering how many different former lives she was scraping away. When she sat up, her back clenched tight as a drum, so she set about stretching.

Kevin Fever slumbered fitfully on the ground, looking for the life of him as if he was never going to wake up. *Trust a raider to sleep the day away.*

When she finished, and her back was as limber as it was going to be, she called to K. Fev to wake up. His eyes opened lazily, and in the strange, orange light of morning, his baby blue peepers took on the hue of the sun, almost as if he looked at her from the depths of two perfect stars.

"Am I still dreaming?" K. Fev asked.

Part of her wanted to go with it, say something like, "Yes, you are dreaming," and then rip her clothes off and spend the morning doing what the animals did. The other part of her thought as soon as she got naked in front of this raider she would be as good as dead, for she knew he was a raider after the previous night's conversation. You couldn't trust a raider, especially not when it came to matters of the heart; raiders ate hearts. Not that her heart was invested in anything K. Fev had to offer.

"If it is a dream, it has to be the most boring dream anyone could ever dream."

"Not if you're in it."

She blushed a little bit, which on her fair skin was a lot. To hide her face, she turned and dug around in her backpack, making a show of arranging things, though there was very little in her bag. "Hurry up," she said. "If we're lucky, we can catch him today."

104

Kevin Fever sighed, and when she heard him make his way to his feet, she turned to look at him, lest he pull his machete free and chop her in the back. She watched him stand on his tiptoes and stretch his own back. The bulge in his leather pants was prominent, and she knew he was at least working with something, you know, if she wanted to go that route. He turned his back to her and pissed into the waste mist, while she studied the shape of his back underneath his faded black T-shirt. Through small rips and holes, she beheld olive-tinted skin.

Then K. Fev turned around, tossed his shoulder pads over his head and tightened the straps. "Ready when you are."

Ajax nodded, searching the ground for the comedian's trail.

"Over here," Kevin called, cocking his head and flashing his perfect smile.

I need to find the comedian fast and get rid of this guy. She was only half aware of this thought, half aware that nothing good could come from her association with Kevin Fever. He was a symbol of temptation in her mind. If the gods were real, as some at The Coop had believed, she would have thought Kevin Fever a test sent by the mad gods, for surely they had gone insane. Crafted to set her blood to boiling and imbued with enough brains to keep him interesting, Kevin Fever was the perfect embodiment of chaos. And currently, she was resisting his charms, resisting her own urges, but it was a losing battle.

At The Coop, love was an orderly thing, not a thing borne from whims and chaos. You didn't just get drunk with someone one night and then go out and bang them behind the chicken coop. Love, and indeed sex, was a prescribed thing. If you were interested in someone, first you checked with their parents. Then, if they gave permission, you would have to prove yourself by undertaking a quest.

Of course, the nature of the quest was a good indicator if someone was interested in you or not. If someone really liked you, they would set you up with an easy quest, something like fetching them a flower or catching them a fish. If they weren't into you, they would send you on an ordeal. Once, Ajax's friend Marvel, one of the most beautiful women in The Coop was courted by Thing, a massive brute of a man with a face that looked like it had been through a cheese grater. Instead of a flower, Marvel tasked Thing with bringing her a sack full of raider heads.

Seeing as how Thing was only a teenager at the time and not able to go out on his own, he had to wait three years until he was able to fulfill the request. In the meantime, Marvel went through a dozen other suitors, all going through the proper channels. However, none of those relationships made it through post-production.

Post-production was the process whereby the parents and the potential mates sat down and discussed the merits of the budding relationship. In order for the relationship to continue, three of the four parties must agree that the relationship could and should continue. Somehow, with Marvel, no one ever seemed to agree. She was difficult to get along with, and very demanding of her lovers' attention, which turned many of her suitors against her. It was one thing to dream and fantasize about a person, but quite another to get close enough to see all of the imperfections of personality and character.

So as time passed, Thing grew older, stronger, training his heart out so when he came of age and was allowed to leave The Coop, he would be ready to fulfill his quest and win the heart of his would-be love.

When Thing came striding back with a lumpy bag of heads, some five years after he had exposed his affinity for Marvel, she could only stand there and accept it. They dated for a while, and at the post-production meeting,

Marvel was the only one who was not interested in Thing's affections. But the other three, seeing that Marvel would do no better than Thing, and that she had already been through most of The Coop's population of viable men and women, agreed this was the best possible match, and from that day forth they went into wide release, and everyone knew about their love and their relationship.

Needless to say, love in The Coop was quite a production, and these thoughts were in the back of her mind. Would her mother approve of K. Fev's seeming interest in her? Would K. Fev ever have the guts to approach The Fury and ask for permission to date her? And if so, what task would she set for him? Something easy? Something impossibly hard?

She wished she were back at The Coop, back under the comforting yolk of rules, routines, and protocols. Out here in the waste, chaos seemed to rule everything, including her heart.

"We gonna go, or what?" Kevin asked.

"Oh, uh. Yeah."

Ajax blushed again. Kevin Fever set off, his machete bouncing against his muscular, leather-clad thigh.

Ajax quivered for a moment and then followed along, cursing her libido.

****

The comedian's tracks were easy to follow. They weren't so much tracks as they were furrows in the ground, lazy steps, the steps of a man on his last legs.

"What are you gonna do if you find this guy dead?"

"I'll return home and report my findings."

"Home, huh? Where's that?"

Ajax pointed in a general direction to the west. She wasn't in the business of telling everyone where The Coop was. It was a large place, but insular. They didn't like guests or visitors, and they rarely took in anyone who had not grown up in The Coop. The knowledge would do nothing for Kevin Fever but leave him out in the cold. In addition, she didn't trust his raider ways.

"What were you doing out here?" Ajax asked.

Kevin shrugged his shoulders. "What's anyone doing out here?"

"That's not an answer."

"It's as much of an answer as you gave me when I asked about your home."

Ajax shrugged. "Fair enough."

"Oh, come on. Don't you want to know about me? I want to know about you."

"What's there to know?"

Kevin laughed, throwing his hands in the air. "You really don't like me, do you?"

Ajax paused, unable to answer for the moment. The truth was part of order, but she felt the pull of chaos. Instead, she chose not to say anything.

"Fine. I'll tell you. I was with a gang, some bad people, not the worst mind you, but not the best. To the south, we ran into some trouble, another gang, badder than us, larger."

Though she devoured every word, Ajax kept her silence and continued studying the ground and the failing tracks of the comedian.

"Things went bad. A lot of people died, mostly my people. I escaped into the night because I didn't want to be on their menu."

"You lose anyone you care about?"

"Lost some people I'll miss, but I wouldn't say I cared about 'em."

"How long were you with them?"

"Long enough."

Ajax scaled a small rise, hoping to spy the comedian ahead, but all she saw was another jagged hill, the comedian's tracks clear among the dirt and rocks.

"What is the point of you?" Ajax asked. The words were out of her mouth before she could stop them.

Kevin Fever, caught off guard, asked, "What do you mean?"

"I mean, you're out here, wandering around, hanging out with raiders, getting chased by raiders. Is that what you want? What's the point of it all?"

"I'm just trying to survive like everyone else."

"But you don't have to kill others to survive."

Kevin Fever shrugged. "People do lots of things to survive. Don't tell me you've never done anything questionable to live."

"My life is my own, and I will protect it, but the same applies to others. One who tries to take a life, they're already dead inside, just as bad as the walking dead. I just put them out of their misery, keep them from taking more lives."

"I wish I could see the world the way you do. It's so easy for you. Good, bad. Chaos, order. Me? My only concern is making it to the next day."

"That's a terrible way to live."

Kevin smiled at her. "I've made it so far. Every day is a good day."

"Even when you're killing someone?"

Kevin looked off in the distance, lost in thought. "Some days are better than others."

Up the rise they climbed. Her thighs and calves burned as they pressed onward and upward. Her heart dropped as she realized she would have to kill Kevin. Her last lustful feelings evaporated at the knowledge. It would be wrong to sleep with a man and then kill him. It was tough living by a code, but that's the way it was.

She didn't talk then. Instead, she readied herself for the deed. Maybe at the top of the next rise, when she had caught her breath, she would put the handsome raider down. Leave him with a nice view of the wasteland as his body dried out in the waste air.

Sadness settled onto her shoulders, making each step feel heavier and heavier. The yoke of order was a heavy yoke to bear, but she would pull it and sow the seeds of healing the world so desperately needed. She would pave the broken road, though she buried her heart underneath it.

Kevin Fever, no longer K. Fev in her mind, walked in front of her as her hand dropped to the mace at her side. One swing. That's all she would need. He was damaged, injured, twisted by the wasteland and its harsh rules for survival.

He could change. Maybe she could change him, make him see the error of his ways.

He is chaos. Her mother's words twisted in her ears. If Kevin Fever ever asked her mother for permission to court Ajax, her mother would laugh in his face, have him drawn and quartered and fed to the chickens.

But I'm not my mother.

But I am my mother's daughter. Her heart and brain warred with each other.

As Kevin Fever reached the top of the rise, he put a hand to his brow to block out the glare of the waste sun. She pulled her mace free.

"Holy shit! You gotta see this!" he said. He turned then and saw her with her mace in her hand.

"What are you doing?" he asked. His eyes grew large and round.

"I'm sorry."

He fumbled at his thigh for his machete, and then she brought the mace down on his head. He crumpled to the ground, and only then did she notice the green valley below. When she looked at the dead man at her feet, blood and brains leaking from his fractured skull, she saw tiny spiders crawling all over his face, that beautiful face. He would be a feast for the spiders. Something ran through her, draining the world of its color and life. Regret. That's what it was.

Numb, she descended into the green valley.

****

All around her, lush green plants grew so fast she could almost hear their roots creeping through the soil. Still gripped in her hand, her mace dotted the green leaves with red spots as she strode down into the valley.

There were two sets of footprints now, crisscrossing the valley floor, and she hoped to find that one of them belonged to the comedian. But the extra set of footprints gave her something to focus on, other than the murder… no, not murder. Order. That's what she had delivered. Order. Just as The Coop demanded. All raiders, all those who would prey on the weak, were agents of Chaos, no matter how handsome they were.

At the nadir of the valley, she met a kindly looking farmer who waited for her, his head bowed and his face hidden by a straw hat that seemed too large for his head.

"Welcome," the man said as she approached.

This was not the comedian. Disappointed, she put her mace away, slamming the handle through the loop on her belt.

"Thank you," she said, her voice steady and even. Inside, she was anything but.

"The land told me there would be two of you."

"Just one," she said.

The man lifted his head and looked into her eyes, squinting. He nodded, his face sad, then he spread his arms wide and beckoned her to a cold campfire. "Come. Eat."

111

In no particular hurry at the moment, Ajax did as she was bid. She needed a rest, and this glorious green valley, though she didn't deserve it, lay heavy with the promise of respite.

As she squatted down, the man said, "My name is Beandick Arnold."

"Ajax."

"I know."

****

"Are you hungry?"

Ajax shook her head and said, "No, but if food is available, I will eat."

"This is wise."

"How much for your food?"

"You have already left your payment in the dirt." The farmer, in his ragged blue overalls, his hands waste-tanned, nodded his head in the direction where she had left Kevin Fever. "There ain't no better fertilizer than the bodies of the dead."

She nodded, though the thought of Kevin Fever rotting in the ground, deflated her spirit even more.

The man, seeing she was unhappy, brought her a selection of fine fruits and vegetables. They were twisted and mutated, not like any produce she had ever seen. She ate without tasting, ignoring the bitter and savage taste of the freakish fruits.

Halfway through her second pomato, she found her voice. "Have you seen him?"

Beandick nodded as he leaned on his elbows, his feet crossed at the ankle, a small piece of straw twirling between his lips. "I seen 'im. Sent him on his way this morning."

Ajax nodded. This was good. It meant she wasn't far behind.

"You seem lost," Beandick said, his squinting eyes staring at the sun through the waste haze high in the sky.

"I have my path."

"Not lost in the world, lost inside."

"Life is not easy."

"No, it ain't."

"Do you have problems with raiders out here?"

"Not so far. But one day I will. Can't keep a place like this a secret forever."

"I won't tell."

Beandick nodded. "I know. T'won't make a difference though. Nothing green can stay. Not in this world. But of course, you found that out today, didn't you?"

Ajax nodded. Indeed she had.

"Are you going after the broken man?"

She nodded.

Beandick twirled the straw in his lips. "It's easy to throw away what's broken. Much harder to fix it."

"You think he can be fixed."

Beandick shrugged. "When it comes to man, there's always a way."

"Did he seem violent to you? Did he seem like a murderer?"

Beandick nodded. "But everyone is these days."

Ajax took another bite of pomato, chewing on the apple-like flesh and spitting the bitter, jelly-covered seeds on the ground. "Everyone? What about you?"

She didn't want to know if Beandick was a killer. He seemed kind and nice in a world where such things seemed to be rarer and rarer with each turn of the moon. But, if he was an agent of chaos, she would have to deal with him, the way she had poor Kevin Fever.

"Everyone," he said, reiterating his point. "Why, just now, I sentenced a man to his potential death. If you should find him, and find him too broken to be fixed, then

113

his blood will be on my hands as surely as it will be on yours."

Ajax accepted the answer. It was satisfactory. She dared not press further, lest Beandick confess to something that demanded justice. She popped the last bite of pomato into her mouth and rose to her feet.

"Thank you for the food."

"Thank you for the fertilizer. Feel free to take more for your journey."

She thanked him again and stuffed her near-empty bag full of the pomatoes. When she was done, she turned to thank Beandick, only to find he had disappeared. Stalking around the green valley, she found the comedian's footprints in the dust. It wouldn't be long now.

Saying goodbye to the green dream behind her, she stepped into the wastes once more. With her feet firmly on the dry, crunchy earth, she spared one last look at the verdant valley, expecting the dream-like place to have disappeared completely. But it was still there, calling to her, begging her to protect it and wander through its cool green leaves and grass.

She stepped into the burnt mists, keeping her eyes on the ground, though she left a part of her heart in the valley behind.

Chapter 10: The Fucks

The comedian strode with new purpose in his step, the nightmares of his collapse playing around the fringes of his mind.

"Say what you will about pomatoes, but fuck do I feel good."

Just wait until you have to go to the bathroom.

"Whatever, Odd."

With new energy and a semi-full belly, he continued his journey, striding through the mists without a care in the world. As he walked, he hummed tunes out loud, tweaking them and twisting the lyrics to make them more appropriate for the world he lived in. He couldn't wait to throw the Fetus Grand into his comedic arsenal.

The sun beamed down on him through the haze, a hot day. With his canteen full, he sang the praises of a man named Beandick as he splashed a precious mouthful of cool, mineral-rich water into his mouth.

The way was easier now, the land sloping downward so he had to turn sideways to keep from tumbling down the slope.

You're not even going to talk about it?

"Talk about what?"

Your memories.

"Nothing to talk about."

Oddrey fell silent, and the comedian tried to walk away from his lie, but the memories came on anyway, clinging to his heels like wet toilet paper. Without warning he was back in the basement. The knife on his hip gripped in his hand.

"No!" he screamed, and he lunged into a half-hearted jog. With the memory of what he'd done playing in his mind, he was blind to the sharp descent of the slope. He stumbled first, then fell, then tumbled down the slope. If it wasn't for the lumpen shape of his body due to his backpack, the piano, and his sword, he would have rolled all the way to the bottom of the hill. On one particular roll, the blade of his sword plunged into the ground, and he found himself leveraged upright, his feet kicking in the air. Like a hanged man, he dangled there as the gritty wind scoured his body.

Behind his goggles, he closed his eyes, and the memories came unbidden.

He unsheathed his knife.

The men ran down the stairs.

"They won't have her."

He sheathed his knife again.

The comedian howled in the real world, the one that didn't care if he lived or died. The one where his daughter no longer existed. He howled his rage, spittle flying from his lips as he cursed the world and the god he knew didn't exist. He cursed the people, the sky, the wind. He cursed everything from the tiniest rock to the sun up above.

****

In the darkness, he heard their boots on the steps. They made it through.

"Daddy," Audrey whimpered.

"It's ok," he said. His hand slid down to his thigh, and he pulled his knife free.

"I won't let them hurt you."

"I want Mommy."

"I know, baby girl. I know."

Thoughts of what the raiders would do to her ran through his head. He knew the world for what it was, a sick place that chewed up innocence and happiness and spat it onto the ground, broken and rotting to return to the earth. These raiders were part of the problem, but he wouldn't let them have her.

116

He knew the spot, where the skull met the spine. As their flashlights came on, he drove the blade home and Audrey spasmed in his lap. "It's alright, Aud. I'll see you soon."

He set his daughter gently on the ground, and then he stood with his knife in his hand, his daughter's blood dripping onto the basement's dusty concrete.

The raiders shone their lights in his face, but he didn't care. There was nothing to speak about now. The best part of him lay cooling on the concrete, and he rushed forward, his knife slashing at faces, at throats. The raiders, trapped on the stairs, stumbled backward, away from his fury, falling over each other to escape the madman in the basement. Their flashlights fell from their hands in their haste, but he didn't need the light to know anything he stabbed was as it should be.

When he was done, they lay there, their blood pooling on the steps. The knife wounds, the slashes, looked too small, not damaging enough for those who had forced him to kill his daughter. *No, she's not dead. Not yet.*

Their weapons lay on the ground. Above he heard more voices calling for their friends, names that meant nothing. Two handguns, silver and clean. He plucked them from the ground after he placed his knife back in its holster. The blade still had his daughter's blood on it. He would never wash it. Though he couldn't take her with him, he could take the blade, make the world right for other people.

He didn't creep up the stairs, he ran full force, and when he burst onto the main floor of the house, the men and one woman turned and looked at him, their eyes big and round, their mouths locked in surprised O's. The mouths he used as targets, and driven by rage and grief, he lifted his two, gun-filled hands and began to squeeze the triggers. Hair, brains, and blood splattered the walls, transforming the peach-colored surfaces into gruesome art. One of the men gurgled at him as the comedian pulled the strap of his machine gun over his face. The metal of the machine gun was cold and heavy.

After a swift kick to the man's jaw that sent teeth sliding across the wooden floor, he pounded up the wooden stairwell leading to the house's second floor. He rushed to a bedroom overlooking the front yard. Out front, he saw a caravan of modified vehicles, vans and trucks, armored and heavy.

He kicked out the window, stuck the barrel of the machine gun through the broken glass, and pulled the trigger. He wasn't wild with his shots. Though he would be perfectly fine dying right then and there, he took aim before he squeezed the trigger, peppering the shocked raiders with bullets. Despite their greater numbers, he murdered a surprising chunk of them before they hopped in their vehicles and drove away, leaving their dead behind because they were pieces of shit.

"All pieces of shit."

He sat in the window of the second floor for a full day before he moved. When he did move, his legs were stiff, but his heart was even stiffer. Sobbing and crying, he shambled through the house, rifling through the gifts of the dead to find anything of value. Guns, ammunition, food, cigars, he took it all and dumped everything in a corner where the blood hadn't pooled. The entire time, he avoided looking at the gaping black rectangle of the basement door that led to his daughter's final resting place.

One by one, he dragged the raiders from the house, beating them and stomping on them as he did so. A stream of curses flew from him, a river of vulgarity, forgotten as soon as the words escaped his mouth. Outside, he felt something pulling at his heart, a string, tight and deadly, wrapped around the beating meat in his chest. That string prevented him from leaving, kept him from running away, and the longer he stayed, waiting for his revenge on the raiders, the tighter the string grew.

In the garage, he found a half-full bottle of lighter fluid and some charcoal briquettes. He built himself a nice little bonfire in the back and threw the raiders on top in an attempt to draw their friends back. He sat out back as the gritty wind scraped his face. When they came, he would kill them. He wouldn't hide behind walls or seek to dodge their bullets. He would walk right at them, guns blazing, until they shot him dead. It was the least he could do.

But they never came… they never came.

****

"Why me!" he shouted, his arms and legs dangling in the air. "Why am I still here!"

He kicked and struggled until the blade of Side-Splitter came free, then he tumbled to the ground on the seat of his pants. He bent over, drool leaking from his mouth, his eyes pinched shut, and he grasped two handfuls of crumbling soil in his gloved hands. He pounded on the dirt, cursing and flailing.

Until he saw the doll head hanging from his jacket.

"Oh. There you are."

Odd did not speak.

"I thought I lost you. I had a dream… a dream that you were gone. Well, I guess it was more of a nightmare really."

Were you scared?

"Nah. Me? Scared?" A half-hearted titter escaped his mouth. "You know me, Odd. I ain't scared of shit, except maybe losing you."

I know.

"You know I love you, right?"

I know. I love you too, Dad.

The comedian pulled his goggles from his face and swiped at his eyes with the military jacket's lapels.

"I love you too, kiddo."

119

The comedian lifted the doll head to his lips and kissed her on the cheek. Sputtering, he spit on the ground. "You need a bath."

That makes two of us.

****

The comedian walked in a daze, slipping in and out of reality. He walked like a man on a mission at times, a man who wished for nothing more than death on others. The oddest thing was sometimes he called Oddrey "Audrey," which didn't seem right to him. It still sounded the same, but… in his head, the spelling was off.

Strange that.

As he walked, something fantastic rose out of the mists, a work of art. He stumbled as great rounded hills rose before him. Beautiful and strange, his first thought was that someone had painted the hills. Lines of color, vermilion, and cornflower, and amber striated the dome protrusions. But the closer he walked, the more obvious it became that the hills were a product of nature and not man. He admired them for a while, his hands massaging his aching back, his sword and his gear at his feet. A good five minutes.

Why don't you take a picture? It'll last longer.

"Oh. Good idea." The comedian mimed like he was holding up a cell phone. "Click." He put the imaginary cell phone away. "That's a good'un. Have to print it out when we get home."

Where's home? Oddrey asked.

"Wherever I am is home for you. Wherever you are is home for me."

You're so cheesy.

"Yeah, well, when you grow up and have kids of your own…"

The comedian studied the hills for another second, not too long, but long enough, then he bent down and plucked his sword and backpack from the desert rocks at his feet, situating them on his aching back. A nice, neat road, all gravel and dust, led through the hills, and he followed it, stopping for a second in a tourist parking lot. A couple of rotted cars sat rusting on their rims, and he pawed through a garbage receptacle, finding the world's oldest dirty diaper and a bottle of water with a drop of liquid still trapped inside. He unscrewed the cap and waited for the water to fall on his tongue. After, he gave the rusted, rotting hulks a quick once over, finding nothing, and then continued on the road.

It had to lead somewhere. Maybe Ike.

****

After three miles, the road ended at an old highway. It was now nothing more than cracked asphalt with tawny scrub grass poking up through the snaking crevices. An ATV might be able to use the road, but nothing less sturdy than that. It looked more like an ancient, dried riverbed than anything a car had once traveled on.

He paralleled the highway, not willing to twist an ankle on the crumbled asphalt. A sign read "itch 6." Many of the letters had faded and peeled, but "itch" still clung stubbornly to the sign.

"6 miles to Itch. Whaddya think about that, Odd?"

It's not another whoretown, is it? I hate those.

"I got no idea. We're just going to have to find out."

Well, if it is another whoretown, stuff me in your backpack. I don't want to see anything.

"Deal."

The comedian whistled a jaunty tune as he walked down the road, the sun above turning the old pavement

121

chunks hot enough to cook an egg. He'd kill a hundred raiders for some eggs right now.

The scenery didn't change as he walked. The world consisted of yellow hills, gritty sand, and stubborn brown grasses which refused to stop existing. The soil baked underneath his boots, and his clumsy feet kicked rocks into parched ditches. But nothing mutated and weird jumped out at him, so that was something.

His earlier optimism and energy had begun to fade, and as he neared the town of Itch, he began to look forward to sleeping in the shade, and hopefully dodging the hottest part of the day.

The cracked asphalt split and a couple of posts, stripped of the road sign they had once supported, were all that marked the exit for "Itch." The comedian took the split, and after a mile, he came around a bend and found the remains of a small town. The first building he came to was an old Post Office. Out front a flagpole still stood the test of time. Gray, frayed ropes clanged against the metal pole in the arid wind. At the top of the flagpole, a desiccated skull hung, long red hair blowing in the breeze.

The post office was little more than a house reappropriated for the once important duty of delivering bills and junk mail. Its ceiling had caved in long ago. Still, he peered through the wreckage to see if he could spot anything worth scavving. Inside, nothing but a few remnants of undelivered letters, rotted and soaked from rains long absent.

Someone is watching, Oddrey said.

The comedian had felt it before Odd said anything, his flighty sixth sense kicking in. As he leaned back, he studied the faded words on the side of the post office, and "Itch" suddenly became "Mitchell." Without tipping off his observers as to his awareness of their presence, he backed away from the post office, smiling at nothing and pretending he was out for a stroll in the park.

122

As he casually took in Mitchell, he noted its layout created something of a choke point. With a row of buildings on either side of the main thoroughfare, there was nowhere to go if something were to happen. Behind the buildings, steep, rocky hills rose. Anyone with a spear or an arrow could easily slay someone trying to scale those cliffs. His only course of action was to suck it up and edge forward. *Besides, I want some fucking shade.* If he got caught out in the burning sun with what little water he had, he was a dead man anyway.

The sword on his back and his bulging muscles were usually enough to ward off lone wasters who might think to attack him. Of course, if there were multiple people, that usually wasn't the case. A gang of raiders would attack for no reason other than if someone died, they would at least be fed for the evening, even if it was one of their friends they had to eat.

He spotted multiple buildings suitable to his purpose. In the end, he chose the general store. A wooden sign, ancient and dry as sunblasted, desert bone read "Wheeler Country Trading Co." Out front, the building had a wooden overhang. It reminded him of the type of building you'd find in an old western. It was probably a nice, kitschy little spot back in the day, when the world still turned and people could do things like buy stupid souvenirs while out on vacation. He walked across the shattered road and paused in front of the store.

"I'll give 'em one chance," he whispered so only Oddrey could hear.

That's so kind of you.

"I know," he hissed. Then he leaned back, opened up his throat, and yelled, "Is anybody here?" His voice echoed off the rocks and storefronts. Anyone who lived in the town, and certainly the people with their eyes boring into his back, would have to hear such a greeting. He waited in the shade of the store's overhanging roof, eyeing the wooden support posts dubiously. A scorpion, small and black, crawled across the concrete sidewalk which had weathered the apocalypse just fine.

No one came out to greet him. No one answered back. No one threatened him. That meant one of two things. They were either cowards, or they were going to try and kill him. Either way, he needed a fucking nap, so he stepped inside the store, pushing open a whitewashed wooden door with ancient, faded fliers plastered to its exterior. One of the fliers caught his attention. A picture, faded to black and white, showed five kittens in a basket, apparently available for adoption. *Cute.* He ripped a couple of the fliers free. Old paper made excellent bum wipe, and while he was usually running so far past E he didn't need to shit for weeks, he could feel the weight of Beandick Arnold's produce churning in his guts.

Pushing inside, he saw the store had been stripped of everything. Bare racks jutted up in the middle of the store, modern, metal, and in stark contrast to the building's old-timey façade. Empty coolers lined the walls, and a smashed cash register lay sideways on the floor, its side bashed in and its drawer yawning open like the broken jaw of a dead raider. He hoped whoever had robbed the place had found something to do with all the money they stole, as most people had stopped using cash for anything other than kindling soon after the bombs fell.

As a rule, most banks in the world were little more than tombs for a forgotten civilization's currency now. One day, a hundred years from now, whatever species took over the planet, say cockatoos, would unearth a bank and rummage through the stacks of fresh paper currency. Perhaps the cockatoomans would decide the white men on the bills were gods or kings. Then they'd squawk loudly, flap their vestigial wings, and eat a bunch of crackers. Yeah. That could happen.

He discovered a small staircase in the back which led up to a rickety balcony overlooking the store. A collection of old-timey furniture, forgotten even before the bombs, sat collecting spiderwebs on the balcony. Suspended among the thick weaves of gray filaments, the dried husks of spiders sat with their legs curled up, surrounded by hundreds of dead insect parts the spiders had feasted upon and left behind. A couple of panels of latticework would allow him to keep an eye on the store from above. He dropped his gear, but for his sword, and then clomped back down the stairs, whistling a jaunty tune. *This is the fun stuff.*

One of the coolers caught his eye, and he let his mind fill in all the shit that should be on the shelves. Milk, soda, orange juice... beer. For a second, he saw it all there, the world coming back to life, the fluorescent lights in the cooler kicking on with a buzz. He imagined opening the door and pulling out a six-pack of some hazy IPA that tasted like hop-filled ass, standing there, letting the cool freezer air wash over him. But then the world flickered back into reality. He took the butt of his sword and smashed the glass case. With his boot, he swept the jagged, glass shards in front of the wooden doorway at the front of the store. Anyone passing through the front would have to walk or jump across the glass. Either way, that would give him enough of a heads-up to get ready to kill.

"It's a shame they didn't want to play nice," the comedian said.

You don't want to play nice either.

"It's been a while."

Can it ever be long enough between kills?

"Eh... maybe." The comedian checked the few back rooms at the rear of the store, finding only evidence of some survivor or such having squatted there a few days. The mummified scat in the corner, the empty wrappers and

125

bottles told him whoever had stayed there had done so long ago. A few back doors, their locks busted, gave him pause.

With the back clear, he returned to the main part of the store and dragged an empty rack over to block off the rear of the shop. He couldn't lock the doors, but he could make it so if someone came in, he would hear them.

After constructing his own version of a spiderweb, he climbed back up to the balcony and rested on the floor, his back leaning against the wall and his head elevated enough so he could turn and see the front door if needed. He slid Rib-Tickler half out of its sheathe and left his sword lying on the ground, the handle within easy grasp.

Then he closed his eyes.

"G'night, partner."

Goodnight.

****

He awoke in darkness. Outside, furtive voices mumbled in the night. Sneaky voices, stab you in the dark voices. He reached down to his side to feel for his sword, but it was no longer there. A weight shifted to his right.

"Who's there?" he hissed.

"Daddy?"

"No!" he shouted. His brain fought against the dream, but this only made it seem more real, his consciousness refusing to allow him to wake from the nightmare.

"Daddy. I'm scared."

"You're dead."

"Why would you say that?" a voice wailed.

He tried to find his way to his feet, but the darkness spun around him until he was on the floor once more.

"Why would you say that!" the voice screamed.

He refused to talk to it, refused to acknowledge… the person.

126

"Why would you say that?"

"Odd, is that you?"

"Why would you say that?"

In the darkness, he closed his eyes, thinking maybe if he went to sleep in this world, he would wake up in the real one, which was the fake one, which was where he wanted to be, standing in front of a crowd, performing, letting the world and its troubles melt away. He wanted to be there so bad, he could taste the breath of the audience as they laughed at one of his ingenious jests.

Their eyes shone in the dark, and he could see the people they really were as his words fell upon them like a spell, lifting them free of the real world and into the one he created with his words.

"Why would you say that?"

Because it's all I have left in this world. I can play songs now, on the Fetus Grand.

"Why would you say that?"

He shouted into the darkness, a primal scream that threatened to burst the dark bars of his imaginary cell.

The voices grew louder and braver at his scream. They knew he was down here, knew she was with him.

"Why would you say that?" the voice in the darkness demanded.

"Because you're dead!" he screamed back.

In the blackness, he heard shards of glass scraping across the floor, and he knew he had to wake up.

"I'm sorry," he said.

Then he opened his eyes.

****

When he came to, it was still daylight outside. The sun had dimmed from a faded basketball to a rotten, hollowed out orange peel, and he knew there was maybe only an hour of light left.

Gently turning his head, he peered through the white lattice in the direction of the front door. It stood open, and sneaky shapes hopped over the glass. Sports equipment, leather. Raiders. Always raiders.

Remembering the absence of his sword in his dream, he felt for the hilt. The pommel, cool and metallic, greeted his anxious fingertips, and he snaked his fingers around the grip of Side-Splitter. Death was in the store; she followed him wherever he went.

He bellowed at them. "Devious fucks! Crawling around like rats!"

On the balcony, he was protected; they could only come at him one at a time. The stairs were too narrow for anything else, even these emaciated raiders. Rather than take the fight to them, he would rile them up until they attempted to force their way up the stairs and to the balcony. Then he would chop them down. His sword would make short work of them, whoever they were.

Below, he heard them whispering to each other.

"How does he know who we are?" one of them asked.

"Maybe we're famous," a woman said in hushed tones.

The comedian stood up, twirling his sword in his hands in the tight space, limbering up his wrists. There was just enough room for him to swing the blade from side to side. But he wouldn't be swinging, he'd be stabbing, keeping the fucks out of reach as they attempted to charge his position. Side-Splitter would sing tonight.

"Come on!" he shouted. "Come and get me!" They charged up the stairs, twisted bits of metal in their hands. The first came fastest, taking the stairs two at a time. The comedian stood at the top of the stairwell, smiling his wolfish grin.

When the first raider reached the middle of the stairwell, the comedian jabbed his sword out and

128

downward and through the man's throat. The raider froze for a second, suspended in the air, his heels teetering on the edge of a step.

From the back of the store, he heard the metal scrape of the rack he had used as a barricade. *More are coming.* He pushed the raider backward, and he slid from the tip of his blade, spraying the comedian's face with blood. The raider toppled backward, taking the woman behind with him. The comedian hopped down the stairs, and while she struggled to get to her feet, he stabbed her in the chest.

She screamed at first, and as her punctured lungs filled up with her own blood, she began to choke and gasp and spit. She would drown on it, and this was fine with the comedian. At the bottom of the stairs, he turned and faced the raiders who came from the rear of the store. With ancient football helmets covering their heads and baseball bats in their hands, they came, though one look at their friends dead on the stairwell tempered their enthusiasm.

"You fucks are dead."

The two raiders looked at each other, surprise on their faces.

"You've heard of us?" a man in a Seattle Seahawks helmet asked, his loincloth flapping and his starvation abs bunching with each syllable.

For a second, the comedian stood confused.

Kill 'em! Oddrey exhorted. She was so bloodthirsty sometimes.

The comedian stepped forward, swiping his blade sideways. The man on the left put up an arm to block the swing, but the sword cleaved through flesh and bone as if it were made of Play-Doh. The raider's forearm dropped to the floor. The other man ducked, dodging the blade, as his raider friend screamed in the early evening. Then the still intact raider turned and ran like the coward he was.

The man with one hand put up his other arm to block the comedian's next swing, and Side-Splitter cleaved more than just his arm this time. The heavy blade, weighing some thirty odd pounds, ripped through his body like it was made of tissue paper. The two halves of the man tumbled sideways. Clearing his mouth of arterial spray, the comedian spit the raider's own blood onto his corpse.

With the back of his hand, he swiped the blood off his goggles and stood ready for the next wave. There was always a next wave. Raider hierarchies being what they were, the first people sent after a man were always expendable and talentless. This was the case here as well. The raiders he had slaughtered had offered no more threat than the common cold.

I can't see, Oddrey said.

"Oh, sorry about that." The comedian looked down and wiped the blood off Oddrey's face.

Did you see the way that guy split in two? Odd asked.

The comedian nodded.

Outside, he heard more voices, but so far, no one had been brave enough to step through the doors of the general store.

He stood stock-still, listening. Bootsteps on concrete. The sound of clanking wood against the side of the building.

Their next move was obvious as it was what he would have done in the same situation. He heard the scratch of steel on flint. Ten strikes.

What is it? Odd asked. Outside, the sound of boots beating dirt away from the building.

"They're gonna burn us out."

It made sense. This building was old, run-down, dry as desert sand. It wouldn't be missed. Better to burn a building than lose any more people. You could bet that everyone still outside was worth something to the raiders.

The comedian held his position, letting the fire catch. Smoke was good. The sound of fire was good. With any luck, when he busted free from the store, they would be too distracted, and he could catch them with their pants down. That's what he hoped at least. The other option was they'd be waiting for him outside with arrows trained on him, ready to fill his body with more holes than a showerhead.

The store's dry wood went up fast while the comedian took the time to climb up into the balcony and gather his possessions.

It had turned dark outside, and through the smoke and the flames, he could see raiders watching him through the windows. Outside, he could hear their hooting and hollering.

There was a heckler outside. The comedian hated hecklers.

"Come on out, waster! We're gonna cook you one way or another!" a deep, bass voice called. It had the tell-tale cadence of the dimwitted, but his raider cronies still chuckled just the same.

"How do you like your fricasseed waster?" the dimwitted man asked his raider compatriots.

"Well done!" another raider responded.

"I like it rare! After you get a couple burns, come on out, waster. I like mine still kickin'."

The comedian muttered, "Oh, I'll be kicking alright."

From there, the situation turned into a waiting game. The comedian rested the tip of his sword on the peeling linoleum, saving his arm-strength for when he'd need it. He closed his eyes, enjoying the play of light on his eyelids as the flames made their way into the store. It was warm, hot even. The smoke filled his nose, and he imagined it was the fine bouquet of a Cuban cigar. He'd never actually had a Cuban cigar, so it was easy to pretend.

As the light swelled brighter, and the heat grew unbearable, he forced himself to maintain his position in the middle of the store. When he smelled his own burnt hair, his eyes snapped open, and he rushed for the front door.

Flames wreathed the exit, but the door itself had yet to catch fire. Still, he knew the wood would be scorching hot, so he lowered his shoulder and busted through the door, knocking it off its hinges. His charge took him outside into the cool night air, and he let the first blessed breath of the evening enter his lungs.

Rolling across the ground, he came up at the feet of a surprised man. With one quick slice, he cut the man's throat with Side-Splitter. He let the blood-soaked tip of the blade drop to the ground, wrapped an arm around the neck of the dying man, and spun him around just before the first crossbow bolt thunked into the raider's chest. Using the dying raider as a human shield, he smiled as three more bolts punctured the man's guts and lungs.

Then he tossed the dead raider away and charged at the nearest attacker. The end of his crossbow was in the ground as he tried to pull back the string of the bow so he could fire off another volley. With one swing, the comedian severed the man's forearms, and the crossbow, hands still wrapped around it, fell into the dust. The comedian grabbed this man around the neck as well, and spun him around as three bolts struck and killed him.

"Crossbows are for cowards!" he called. "You wanna kill me, you're gonna have to get up close and personal."

"Stop!" a woman called.

The man in the comedian's arms flailed, crying and screaming. His arms waved in the air, blood spraying from the stumps. He only had a minute or so to live.

"I haven't even started," the comedian called back to the woman.

132

She stepped out of the darkness, walking through the smoke like something out of an action movie. Her long, red hair, wavy and filthy, flowed in the wind. She was dressed rather plainly for a raider, but the fact that everyone had stopped when she commanded told him everything he needed to know.

"Righteous warrior. You've already proved your prowess. There's no reason to continue to fight."

"I'm not a warrior, and I'm sure as fuck not righteous."

"Be that as it may," the woman continued, "you have slayed several of us tonight. We could use a man like you."

"No one 'uses' a man like me."

"You would fight to the death?"

She was pretty, her voice softer than he would have expected, but if she was running this bunch, you knew one night you'd wake up with a knife in your ribs… probably your own. But still, she was kind of hot.

Keep it in your pants, Odd said.

"I fight to live."

"Then come. Fight to live with us. Our man said you've already heard of us. Our gang is known across the wastes."

"I don't know you. Your man was wrong."

"But surely, you must have heard of us. We're The Fucks."

At this, the comedian laughed. The man in his arms sagged, his life gone for good. "The Fucks, huh? And what's your deal? What sort of weird, sexual fetishes are you guys into? Raiders like you are always doing weird shit to each other."

"We do not have any weird sexual fetishes. We're just The Fucks. I'm Mother Fuck."

The comedian couldn't help but laugh at this. "You're kidding me." The comedian shook the body he held up. "I know this guy's name. He's Dead Fuck."

Mother Fuck smiled at him, a parent's patient smile for a precocious child who would soon learn a lesson. "Clever too. How is it that you're not running your own gang?"

"Maybe because I don't give a shit about anyone else. I'm a bit of a misanthrope in that way. Now you fuckin' Fucks can just fuck off and leave me the fuck alone."

The raider leader smiled at him, her thin lips looping upward. "If that's the way it has to be." She nodded at him out of respect, turned her back, and waved her raiders forward. They came screaming, several crossbow bolts whistled past his head.

With the crossbows used up, he threw Dead Fuck into the dirt and sprinted up the main road, dodging behind the nearest building before another volley of crossbow bolts thunked into the ancient wood. The raiders behind screamed obscenities at him, nothing original, nothing he could use in his show.

He smiled in the darkness as the light of the fire faded away, replaced by the glowing green light of the sky above.

All in all, he was having a pretty good time.

****

He bashed his way into a building, a bed and breakfast type place. The ancient door splintered into pieces as soon as he lowered his shoulder.

He backed into a lobby, kitschy and wooden. The space was small, too small for Side-Splitter. He leaned his massive sword against the wall and pulled Rib-Tickler free.

134

His trusty hunting knife, covered in the blood of his—nevermind—and the poison of a sand snake.

A man stumbled over the splintered remains of the wooden door, his grin splitting his face in half, his eyes as wide as could be to see in the dim room. His hair, long and greasy, hung down over half his face. In his hand, he held a knife much like the comedian's own.

"Boy, you Fucks never give up, do ya? What's your name, Dumb Fuck?"

For some reason this infuriated the man, and he charged at the comedian, lashing out at him with his knife. The blade whistled through the air, and the comedian had to leap backwards and suck in his gut to avoid being disemboweled. At the same time, he brought his own knife down on the man's wrist, where it clanged off a metal bracer the man had fashioned from a rusty street sign.

His opponent spun, presenting his vulnerable back to the comedian for just a second, but the comedian didn't take the bait. As the man twisted around, the greasy man jabbed his knife straight at the comedian's eye. The comedian dodged, letting the raider's momentum take his blade past his head. In a flash, he stepped on the tip of the man's boot, pinning the spinning madman to the ground. A sharp movement brought the comedian's head up, and the top of his skull crunched into the man's nose, obliterating it.

Staggered and bleeding from his crooked nose, the man fell to the ground, his knife falling from his hand and clattering to the wooden boards. Without pausing, the comedian straddled the man's chest and raised Rib-Tickler over his head. He brought the blade downward, but the man caught his wrists in time.

The raider wasn't smiling now. Not by a long shot. His greasy hair spread on the floor behind him, his face locked in a grimace as the tip of the comedian's knife descended centimeter by centimeter, aiming for a spot in the hollow of the man's throat.

The raider could see which way it was going to go, but still he fought, trying to resist the strength of the comedian. But he was no match for the funnyman's strength. The blade tip inched lower and lower, as inevitable as the sunset.

"Oh, God," the raider grunted through clenched teeth, his own demise playing out in his mind.

"There is no god," the comedian said.

The tip of his knife touched the man's throat, split the skin and then plunged even deeper. The man kicked and bucked underneath the comedian's hips, and then the poison on the blade hit his bloodstream.

His back arched violently, throwing the comedian off. As the raider's body spasmed and convulsed, the comedian turned his back on the man, leaving him to his painful death. The wound he had given the man would not be fatal on its own, but the poison on his blade would finish the job.

Outside, he heard the voices of more Fucks, calling to each other as they searched the abandoned buildings of the town of Mitchell. They wanted to find him, to kill him and eat him.

After retrieving his sword, he stepped over the corpse on the floor, the corpse stiff and contracted from his hands down to his toes.

He stepped out into the green-tinged darkness. Moving silently, he ran, stooped and low, for the edge of town. Though a part of him wanted to kill them all, he didn't have the time or the energy. Besides, he had other things to do.

"He's over here!" a woman called, her voice thick and raspy.

"Fuck." The comedian ran on, his thighs burning. "Time for some Kevin McCallister shit."

Chapter 11: McCallister-Style

Filthy Fuck, Mother Fuck's 2nd Lieutenant, or 3rd maybe... no wait. He was fifth now. Whatever. Filthy Fuck, thus named because of his penchant for dirt baths in lieu of water, swore he saw the big man go running inside this house. He knew the house, had pleasured himself there for days one time, left his mark drying on the drywall.

If he got this guy, Mother Fuck would have to recognize his brilliance, maybe give him a promotion. A promotion meant good things; it meant a choice cut when the meat was ready. No more intestines and toes for him. Pecs and biceps, that would be good enough. Mother Fuck always took the rump bits for herself, but he could maybe swing the pecs or biceps if he pulled this off.

He stepped into the darkness.

"I'm upstairs you useless Fuck," a voice called.

"Ha! Shows what you know, waste rat. You already killed Useless Fuck. I'm Filthy Fuck, and I'm gonna be your doom."

"Oooh, I'm shaking in my boots," the voice called from upstairs.

Filthy Fuck hefted the disassembled arm of a papercutter in his hand. It was an ok weapon, solid, and though it wouldn't cut through a man's arms the way his prey's sword might, a good chop to the head would split skin and bone just the same.

"Pecs and 'ceps, here I come."

He walked up the stairs, moving slow, in case the deadly waster should come rushing at him. He hadn't always been a raider, hadn't always been filthy either. Back in the day, he used to wake up and take a shower every single morning, couldn't leave the house without one. But that was a long time ago, before he had developed a taste for the greatest meat in the land. It wasn't even about survival for him anymore; it was about the taste. Long pig was so much better than anything he had ever eaten, and though his hands shook, and his brain didn't work all that good anymore, he still wanted more, and this long piggy had pecs and ceps like no one he'd seen since before the fall of man.

Up the stairs he went, drool running down his dirty chin, creating dark brown tracks in the muck that covered his body.

"I'm coming for you, piggy!" he called. Then he oinked like a pig, wrinkling his nose and sucking in air. A bit of saliva went down the wrong way, and he began to cough. *Not a cool way to kill anyone. Not at all. In fact, it's fucking embarrassing.* It was either him or the long pig now.

He stepped on the last step, and hot pain shot through his foot. His boots, ancient Uggs he had pried off some pretty man in a vault in the east, were boots in name only. The soles had been worn thin enough, so he felt every rock when walking out in the desert. *But they looked so cool!*

This was the thought in his head as he lifted his foot up instinctively to pull out the offending item causing him such pain. In doing so, he leaned backward, overbalanced, and then tumbled down the stairs, rattling and banging his body off the wooden steps. He felt something break in his arm, cracked his jaw on another step, and his neck twisted at an awkward angle as he came to a rest at the bottom of the stairs.

With his last strength, he lifted his leg so he could examine the bottom of his foot. There was something there, a small thing, shiny and metallic. With his one working arm, he fumbled at the item, and in the feeble light shining through the building's dingy windows, he was just able to make out the pointed end of a small, shiny screw in his fingertips.

"That's mine!" a voice roared, and when he looked up again, his papercutter, his super-cool weapon that made him different from all of the other Fucks, was flying at his face. It landed with a painful thunk between his eyes. His eyes crossed, trying to see the damage the papercutter blade had done, but it was too dark. His eyes wouldn't uncross, and just before he died, he felt someone pry the screw from his fingers and hop over his body.

****

Fuck Buddy heard the scream coming from the house. He scanned the area, saw he was the only person in sight.

"Shit," he said to himself. This guy was a stone-cold killer. They should have known just from the sword. Big as an airplane propeller, a pushover didn't walk around with a sword that size unless they knew how to use it, and they certainly didn't carry it across the wastes and through the slow sands.

On the other hand, if he didn't go in and find the guy, at least make some sort of effort, Mother Fuck would have his head, probably with a side of waste tubers and some poached crunch grass.

Fuck Buddy hadn't always been called such. Once, he had been a man named Claude, a plain sort who liked to sit around and get blazed with his buddies and watch soccer games on the weekend. But the world had changed, and that man, Claude, a good enough name, had been left behind.

Oh, he had tried to get everyone to call him Claude, but The Fucks had a theme going. They had to stick with it. To go against the theme of a raider gang was an affront that could not be overlooked. So, he had donned a goalie helmet, found some gloves and cut the fingers off, and tasted his first piece of human flesh. He hated it. Sour and not right, he felt bad every time he ate something that had used to be just like him. Oh, he didn't feel morally bad about it, but physically bad.

Human didn't have the appeal to him that it did for the others. He'd seen the old timers, the people who had been dining on long pig for years. He saw them shake, their nerves and brains destroyed by cannibalism. Human was poison, but sometimes it was all one had available. Anything, you name it, and he would eat it. He'd rather eat the boogers out of a dead man's nose than take another bite of human meat.

But not the others. They seemed to think they were on short time anyway, that their lives could be over tomorrow morning, and who was to say they wouldn't be? Shit, an evercrack could open up underneath him right now while he stood around thinking about it.

"You see anything?" a voice asked.

Fuck... Titty Fuck to be exact. He sighed to himself and said, "I think he's in here."

"Well, what are you waiting for?" Titty Fuck asked. Despite her name, she was not particularly well-endowed in that area. Though her name implied all sorts of carnal delights, he would probably turn her down if she propositioned him. Her face was equine in nature, angular, frightful. When she smiled, her teeth shone black in the radglow.

Every inch of her body was covered in dirt, and the smell emanating from her was something he could only describe as rancid, as if somewhere in her body, she was rotting to death. Her hands shook, and her gray-red hair fell in clownish tangles about her head.

But, they had been running out of names. There were so many different ways to use the word fuck, they had thought they would never run out of names. But it turns out, they had gone through dozens of them, and no one felt like recycling names, so Titty Fuck she was.

"You going in or not?" she asked.

He nodded his head. Pretending he was braver than he was, he pushed open the door to the shack, a two-story affair, creaky and ready to collapse. "I'll take the top, you take the bottom," he said.

Her moppish hair shook as she nodded, and he edged inside, expecting the rusted hinges on the door to squeak in protest. But he was in luck; the door didn't make a sound. Fuck Buddy stepped lightly across the wooden floorboards, heading for the staircase. Titty Fuck branched off, a machete constructed from a ground-down mile-post marker in her hands.

Good luck. He wished her well, not because he cared for her, but because if she got lucky, that meant he wouldn't have to fight the giant man. Truth be told, he didn't care if the guy lived or died. He didn't care if any of his raider buddies lived or died either. He only cared about himself, and that was the way he liked it. If Titty Fuck hadn't stumbled along to find him, he might have walked right out of town. Better to live another day as a coward than die right now as a hero.

But she *had* found him, and so he climbed the stairs to the second floor, keeping his feet to the edges of the steps. In his experience, these tended to creak a whole lot less. As he thought it, he heard a noise from one of the rooms above, a squeaking, strange sound.

Maybe it's just a rat. Rats is good eatin'. With things looking up, he managed to make it to the second-floor landing without giving himself away. He paused there, listening, straining his ears for the sound he'd heard before... there it was. A low squeak as of wet rubber against a wooden floor.

I got you now. Fuck Buddy stepped up to the door, licking his dry, cracked lips. *Throw it open or go in nice and slow, now that is the question.* In the end, he figured the big man would be waiting for him, his eyes on the door.

141

Maybe he could take him by surprise. Also, if he threw the door open, maybe Titty Fuck would hear him and come running.

He took a deep steadying breath, reared back, and kicked the door open with his boot. It crashed inwards. *Bang!*

Fuck Buddy jumped, his heart leaping into his chest, and then he dove backwards. "He's got a gun!"

Crawling on the ground, he backed away from the door until his hand brushed against the smooth leather of a boot tip. He looked up, hoping to see Titty Fuck's hideous black teeth. Instead, he saw the big man smiling down at him, his eyes hidden behind black goggles. His perfect white teeth were a far cry from Titty Fuck's, and then the man raised something thin and flat into the air. Fuck Buddy had just enough time to realize it was a sword, and then the man drove it downward between his neck and the spot where his spine met. His world rocked, rolling on its side, and he closed his eyes lest he see his own body.

****

Titty Fuck heard the commotion above, but by the time she reached the stairs, she saw nothing but the decapitated body of Fuck Buddy.

We'll eat well tonight.

As one of the few female members of The Fucks, she knew she had to represent. The men were always acting like they ran the damn place, grumbling and mumbling all the time about having to give a fair share to her. They were bigger, stronger, they needed more food. Maybe this was true, but she had brought more to the table than most of them. She would do so again. Tonight, they would feast, and no one would complain about the size of their portion. There were plenty of bodies to go around at this point, but she wanted to taste the waster.

She'd seen his body when he'd come in. Thick and muscular, there was a lot of good flesh on that body, certainly more so than someone like Fuck Buddy. As she crept up the steps to the second floor, she scanned the ground, saw half a bloody footprint leading into a room, and knew that's where the big man had gone.

Poor Buddy. She had known he wasn't cut out for this world from the day she met him. But bodies was bodies, and a raider gang without enough bodies was doomed to break apart eventually. You needed people like Buddy, scrawny and weak. He was good for ripping on, which eased the machismo of the more testosterone-fueled members of the gang. A weakling like Buddy allowed those people to let off some steam. The best thing about Buddy was he didn't fight back, except when he tried to get everyone to call him Claude. But Fuck Claude didn't have the right ring to it.

With Fuck Buddy gone, she supposed Butt Fuck would become the resident whipping boy. Better than her, that was for sure.

Titty Fuck kicked off her boots at the top of the stairs, her fungaloid feet assaulting her nose with a stench she could only barely stand. Padding softly across the wooden floor, she came to stand in front of it, her bare foot stepping on the bloody footprint. With a quivering hand, she reached out for the door handle. Her palsied hand shook against the latch, and she had to concentrate to keep from giving herself away. She pressed down, and then pushed the door open.

Suddenly, the door was pulled from her hand, and she was greeted by the smiling face of a madman. She raised her sharpened road sign into the air, and then it went even higher as she was lifted off her feet. The big man's hands wrapped around her neck, squeezing the life out of her. The sign grew heavy in her hands, and she tried to swing at him, but the old sign, dulled on bone and skull over the years, did not penetrate the big man's heavy jacket.

Just when she thought she was going to die, the big man looked at her and said, "I hate to do this to ya, but I already kinda started. I got a bit goin'. Gotta finish the job. Right, Odd?"

He nodded at something, set Titty Fuck down on her feet, and then spun her around. She had a moment to see a sock with a hole in the toe flash before her eyes, and then she was being choked to death by that very same sock.

****

The comedian let the woman fall to the floor. A sock with a hole in it, a shiny screw, and a yellow balloon. He'd done it... Kevin McCallister style.

Shame about the balloon, Audrey said.

"Yeah." It was a shame. He had rigged it up to burst when the raider opened the door, simulating a gunshot. Now it was nothing but splintered rubber fragments on the floor.

The comedian packed up his gear, patted down the two new corpses, and took anything of worth, down to the buttons on their sleeves. Then he decided to skip town.

Chapter 12: Catching Up

At the end of a long day of marching through beautiful hills, so colorful they looked like an artist's drawing, Ajax came to a road.

Her day had been uneventful, hot but boring.

After she had come to a highway and seen the sign for the town of Itch, she decided to make camp.

She felt confident she would catch the comedian the next day. If not then, the day after that for sure.

As she lay down in the dirt, wrapping her cloak tight around herself, she looked up at the sky. Orange. It was orange. Odd.

Rubbing her eyes, she sat up, the day's march still heavy in her lower back and the soles of her feet. She scanned the sky… and then saw it wasn't the sky that was orange, but some light in the distance reflecting off the filth in the air.

Fire. Something burned in the town of Itch. She sighed deeply, knowing her night was far from over. Whatever was happening in that town, she knew it must be a product of the comedian's presence. His chaos showed itself once more, and she resigned herself to the fact he would have to be put out of the world's misery.

Groaning, she pushed herself to her feet and began the trudge to town, the light growing brighter, smoke rising into the air on inky black plumes.

****

In the dark of night, it was easy to find the source of the light. A building, old, mostly wood construction, was in full flame. As she stood there, the roof of the building crashed in upon itself, sending up a cloud of fireflies that floated through the air and landed on the other buildings

145

that were dry as bone. If the wind blew just right, the town of Itch could be gone in a matter of hours, but that wasn't her concern. Her concern was for the citizens of the town.

She scanned the flame-lit shadows, noting a few shapes slumped upon the ground. Walking over, she grabbed a man by his bootheel and dragged him into the firelight.

Raider. Shit.

Ajax knew she had enough on the comedian to kick the chicken, but if raiders were involved, there would be a lot of order to establish. Depending on the numbers, it might be more than she could handle. But she had yet to shy away from a fight, although most times, she had a friend or two guarding her back.

The raider's bootheel thumped to the ground, and she wiped the carnivorous ants from her hands. Dropping into a crouch, she clung to the shadows of the buildings, moving through the town more cautiously. It wasn't fear of the raiders that drove her chariness. Oh sure, she'd seen the crossbow bolts dotting the man's body, but that didn't concern her. Underneath her cloak and her tabard—not a shirt—she had a length of metal armor, each ring lovingly bent and curled by blacksmiths at The Coop. While the chainmail might not stop a crossbow bolt completely, it would keep them from plunging deep into her body. No, her fear and caution came from the fact that she wanted to judge whether or not the comedian was what he said he was. Was he a plain comedian as he insisted, or the cold-blooded murderer she had always suspected? Definitive proof, her own eyes seeing the comedian in action, would go a long way toward satisfying her own need for justice. Mistakes were known to happen in the wastes, and if she could be a hundred-percent sure, that would be a good thing.

So far, he had left in his wake one body, a raider to be sure, but the way he had left him—bound to a tree with a

146

bungee cord, his face pulled into a macabre smile—that was enough to pass judgment on him. These other raiders though, they were agents of chaos, and their deaths were approved.

"Look thrice, slice twice," The Coop's master-at-arms always said.

"What the fuck is thrice?" Thing had asked upon first hearing the phrase. Ajax had shrugged, not knowing the answer, though she had come to learn it meant three times, although why he didn't just say 'Look three times' instead of 'look thrice' was a mystery to her. Still, the lesson had stuck with her.

You couldn't undo a mace to the skull. And if a Chicken Kicker got it wrong… well, then they were just as bad as the raiders they hunted, right?

With her cloak pulled over her head to hide her sunburnt skin, she ducked low and moved swift across the dry soil of Itch. Underneath her boot heels, unseen, crawling insects crunched, along with the husks of long dead grass. She ducked into the shadows of a building whose roof smoldered. It too would go up in flames in no time. *Who set the fire? The comedian or the raiders?* The raiders would have to be idiots to bring fire into this tinderbox, but most raiders she had encountered were no brighter than the red-orange dullness of the moon above.

Quickening her pace, she walked down the length of the building, careful to duck underneath the broken windows and leap across doorways lest someone waited in ambush.

She was close. Her mission was almost complete, and then she could go back to The Coop. Though she found the freedom of this world intoxicating, she understood this as the influence of chaos. Her interactions with Kevin Fever and Beandick Arnold had shown her as much. Chicken Kickers were not meant to be out in the wastes by themselves. Without someone pure and uncorrupted by

147

your side, it was all too easy to take the path of least resistance, and that path led to ruin, of the world and the soul. No, Ajax needed to finish this job and go home as soon as possible. They would be glad to see her. Though she suspected when she told her tale, the truth of it, down to her own thoughts and feelings, they might not be as glad to have her back. But that was order, sometimes hard and difficult, but always worth it in the end. Better to air your dirty laundry than to ball it up and stuff it under the bed to molder and rot.

Cackling broke the relative quiet of the night, a woman's cackling. It was seldom one heard a woman cackling in the waste. Screaming, sure. Groaning in pain, all the time. But laughing? Never.

She picked up the pace, sure that where the laughing was, she would find the comedian—not because he was funny mind you, but because someone was most likely getting ready to take down a legend before it had even grown, for she knew that was what the comedian was.

Like the great Smokestack Sam, the comedian was destined for big things. Smokestack Sam, the man who almost put Alabama back together, had been a mountain of a man, born in a bubble camp. Of course, he had failed and ended up plunging the entire state into chaos when he was assassinated. The comedian had the same potential. Were he to find some followers, some people willing to sacrifice their lives for him, he would be a dangerous man indeed, especially considering his nomadic lifestyle. Everywhere he went, he would sow the seeds of chaos, leaving growing tendrils of destruction in his footsteps.

An ember fluttered by her face, landing in the dust where it died. The comedian was like that ember. Give him enough time, and he'd land on a building, burn it down, and continue onto the next place until there was nothing left.

Ducking between two houses, she stooped low, trying to avoid the nightglow as much as possible.

The creak of leather in the shadows was the only warning she had. Without hesitation, she dove to the ground. The whistle of something flew over her head as she hit the dirt, and then she was up, charging into the darkness with her mace in her hands.

"Fuck," a voice whispered, and by the sound of the voice, she knew the man struggled to cock his crossbow again. She swung her mace at the shadowy spot whence the voice had come. The crunch of bone and the squish of flesh told her the tale. A weight fell to the ground, and a man tumbled into the dirt. He could still be alive, so she knelt onto the ground, felt around for the roundness of his skull, and then delivered several more blows to his cranium. When she stood up, the knees of her pants were sticky with the raider's blood, but she was sure of his fate at least.

Not wishing to be skewered by an unseen crossbowman in the night, she stepped into the abandoned building whose shadow the crossbowman had been hiding in. The interior was dark, dusty, and reeked of human waste. She didn't know why, with an entire world outside to use as a jakes, raiders chose to shit in the corner, but this place had the tell-tale smell of a raider hole.

As she let her eyes adjust to the dim interior, she spotted a set of stairs leading up to a second floor. Every step she took was unbearably loud, the brittle steps below her threatening to snap in half with each one she climbed. On the second floor, she clung close to the wall, not trusting the ancient boards to hold her weight. She knelt low, her cloak masking her face as she crept toward a window.

Outside, she could see the comedian on his knees, a smile on his face. His weapons lay on the ground, and a woman rummaged through his backpack.

"You gave us a hard chase," the woman said. "You killed a lot of us. But, I'm going to give you one last

149

chance. Join us. Fight with us, and I guarantee you the best cuts of meat."

The comedian sat on his knees and said nothing.

"No? Nothing to say?" the woman began. "Well, let me tell you who we are, maybe that'll change your mind. You see, we're not ordinary raiders. We don't go around doing sexual things to people. We're just here to survive. When we're not just surviving though, we're living our lives in this town. It's a simple life, but it's fine. The weather is nice, there's no waste rain, the waste fog doesn't come here, and there are towns, no more than a day's walk from here, that are ripe for raiding. So join us… become a Fuck."

"I've been a fuck for most of my life," the comedian said.

At this, the raider woman laughed. "He's funny," she said to her crew. "Got a sense of humor this one. We'll call you Funny Fuck. How about it?"

"Why would I join you? As far as I can tell, you're just like all the raiders out there."

At this, the female raider reared back, and Ajax could tell the comedian had offended her. In the night, sparks rained down upon them. Another building had gone up in the town of Itch.

"You should join us because we're different. Look around, none of us are alike. Everyone one of us is different. Look, right there, Fat Fuck has fingerless gloves, except for the pinky fingers. Butt Fuck, he wears corduroy pants and his gloves still have the middle finger on them. Look at me! I wear a button up shirt! And the glove of my right hand still has ALL of its fingers! All of them!"

The comedian laughed then. "You think you're different because of your clothes? No one gives a fuck about your clothes. No one cares what fingers you've cut off your gloves. You're still, dirty, dick-eating cannibals with nothing more to offer in this world than a quick death."

150

"So that's a no?"

"That's a no."

The raider woman nodded, and the other raiders pulled their weapons free.

"I admire your conviction," the woman said. "See? That's different, right? Would you ever hear another raider say that?"

"I've heard it before, from the lips of a thousand raiders. All your squeals sound the same, Mother Fuck."

Ajax, knowing the end was coming, couldn't help herself; she burst through the glass window and slid down the pitched roof, tumbling and rolling out of control. In mid-air, she righted herself and landed upon her feet, her mace already in her hand.

The raiders turned to look at her, shocked by her entrance. Sparks fell all around, and the wind picked up, swirling the glowing embers into a fiery cyclone. Their mouths agape, none of the raiders noticed the comedian rising to his feet, his blade in his hand.

"Who the fuck—

Mother Fuck's question was interrupted by the blade of the comedian's sword. Blood poured down her throat, and her right hand, encased in a glove that still had all of its fingers, reached up to paw at the air as her head fell off.

From there, the battle was truly begun.

Chapter 13: Putting Fucks in the Ground

With Mother Fuck distracted, the comedian picked up Side-Splitter, the knuckles of his fingerless gloves scraping across the deadpan dirt of Mitchell. He stood, enjoying the weight of the sword in his hands. He pulled his arms back, looking like an old-timey baseball player. How long had it been since someone played a game of baseball? *Years? Decades?*

It didn't matter to him really. The thought was only a curiosity.

His arms sprung to life, and he swung for the fences as they used to say. The force of his swing cleaved through the neck of Mother Fuck, and her head popped into the air, spinning, her long hair splaying out in a pinwheel fashion as her skull did a somersault. He admired it for a moment, fixing the image in his mind, so he could replay it later. His memories of raider deaths kept him warm on cold nights.

From there, the battle was truly engaged. The Fucks swarmed around him, their fingerless gloves wrapped around their wasteland weaponry. Here a meat clever, there a machete, here a length of rebar turned into deadly steel knuckles. He didn't eye the people so much as he eyed their weapons.

Dodging and ducking, he began to dance. It was the only dance he knew, the dance of life and death. Laughing, he dodged a machete aimed at his neck. Then he spun, his sword held point down to block the punch of a set of steel, rebar knuckles. Afterward, he sprang backward to engage another partner, this one wielding a baseball bat wrapped in razor wire—because why not?

A baseball bat—sure, that's a fine weapon, but a baseball bat wrapped in razor wire? Now that's a work of art.

152

The bat clanged off the edge of Side-Splitter, the razor wire scraping down its length and sending more sparks into the night.

From the corner of his eye, he saw the woman, the Chicken Kicker, dealing swift, blunt justice to the raiders. She faced greater numbers than he did. Apparently, they had figured her for an easy mark. By the amount of gore dripping from the end of her mace, they had been sorely mistaken.

The comedian stepped to the side, his feet crossing over each other at the ankles, as nimble as any ballerina who ever graced the stage, and he spun, pirouetting and bringing his sword across the chest of the woman with the razor-wire baseball bat. His wrists throbbed from the impact as the vibrations traveled up the length of his sword, and Side-Splitter opened a wound that began at the woman's collarbone and drove into her breast. A wash of hot, blood spray splashed his face, tinting the world red through his goggles.

Quickly, he swiped at the lenses with the back of his hand, and at the last second, he brought the sword up to fend off the vicious chop of a meat cleaver. The man wielding it wore a floppy chef's hat, and the comedian wondered if he was in fact the raider's chef, or if he just liked to play dress up.

The chef was quick; he'd give him that. His arm flew backward and forward, slicing through the air and sending showers of sparks shooting off into the night every time the cleaver clanged off the comedian's blade. He was perhaps too fast, and the comedian couldn't find an opening in his assault. The best he could do was hope for the man to tire himself out.

From behind, he heard a whistle of air, and he ducked. A machete sailed through the spot where the funnyman's head had been, and a man with a mohawk overbalanced, surprised at the lack of resistance.

With his arms flailing in the air, mohawk man tumbled into the chef, and the comedian speared Mr. Mohawk through the back, pulling Side-Splitter free and dancing away, lest the chaos of the raider knot wash over him.

Spacing is important. One mustn't let them tighten the noose.

Puffs of dust, rich with radioactive isotopes, sprang upward, and as the chef disentangled himself from the mohawk man, the raider fell to the ground, reaching for his back, as if he could stop the flow of blood with his hands alone. His feet thumped in the dirt, sending up more dust, and the chef, infuriated, his eyebrows thick, his fingers thicker, sprinted at the comedian, his cleaver gleaming in the radglow.

"Cook Fuck? Is that your name?" the comedian asked.

The chef didn't pause to answer, but came on, picking up right where he left off, swipin' and choppin' and hackin' and bobbin'. They danced together, the comedian and the chef, dancing to an improvisational tune, like musicians playing jazz. The comedian hated jazz, loathed it with every fiber of his being. *It's just pretentious fuckers goofing about.*

"Chef Fuck?" the comedian asked.

The chef seemed to become more and more enraged by the comedian's questions, and his blows came faster and furiouser, like a sequel to a franchise that should have ended long ago.

The kid with the rebar knuckles, for he was no older than a teenager, tried to swoop in behind him. The comedian would bet the kid had never even seen a Fast and Furious movie. Some people have all the luck.

"What about you?" he asked, dancing backwards, his sword held upright between him and the chef and the kid with the knuckles. "They call you Knuckle Fuck?"

"Shut up!" the chef yelled, obviously annoyed the comedian wasn't taking the fight as seriously as he was.

The chef came on, leaping into the air and lashing out with his cleaver. It became a flash of silver, like the gleaming sides of a fish in a clear river on a sunny day, darting this way and that, only to disappear and reappear in a different place altogether. The comedian's wrists were starting to tire, and the sword in his hands grew heavier by the second.

He backed up and waited for the next rush from the chef, while the knuckles kid stalked around his side looking to flank him. As the chef came onward, the comedian tossed Side-Splitter in the air. The sudden movement caught the chef by surprise, and though in his head he knew he shouldn't track the movement of the sword in the sky, the chef did it anyway. Instinct, reflexes, his greatest gifts as a fighter, took ahold of him, and his head tilted backward, his eyes locked on the broad blade of the sword as it rose into the air, twirling gently, its length lit by the geyser of flames that Mitchell had become.

Paler than the rest of the chef's filthy body, he exposed his throat, covered in a layer of scruffy beard. The comedian's hands moved, flashing like lightning in a dry storm. He reached inside his coat, grasped the edge of Last Laugh, a six-pointed shuriken. With a flick of the wrist, he sent the shuriken flying, spinning across the space between himself and the chef.

But he didn't have time to watch his throw, to see if the shuriken struck the chef in that stupid throat of his. Of course, he didn't need to watch it with his eyes. He knew the throw had been on point. A *thunk* and a wet gurgle confirmed his confidence. The rebar boy was coming, and though he had chosen a stupid weapon, a length of rebar bent so that his fist could slide through them, one punch from those suckers could do some serious damage.

But he was a kid, and he was dumb like all kids. This one even dumber, as he had missed out on all the things that made modern man intelligent—movies, tv shows, crime scene procedurals, Sesame Street. This kid had been born after the apocalypse, the poor bastard, and he knew about as much about the world before as the comedian knew about not being funny—which is to say very little.

The kid, overconfident, his yellow teeth bared in a smile, rushed at the comedian with his arm cocked, ready to unleash an epic punch that would cave in the side of the comedian's head. Of course, that punch never came. As the kid closed within punching distance, the comedian's hand snaked down to Rib-Tickler, pulled it from the sheathe on his thigh, and then he drove it up under the kid's throat, through the layer of fuzzy beard that grew like moss on an old peach, through the skin, through the soft tissue of his tongue, up through his palette, through the skinny bones of the interior skull and straight into the boy's brain. He jittered at the end of his knife, and the comedian shoved him in the chest, while pulling Rib-Tickler free.

The boy's boots rattled in the dirt, and the comedian couldn't tell if it was because of the poison on his blade or because he had put a neat vent in the boy's brain.

With the kid down, he had time to survey the battlefield.

Across the way, bodies lay in the dirt, blood pooling on the soil. Smoke billowed throughout the city, ashes floating through the air. The woman danced as the comedian had done. Her distraction had pulled him from the brink of death, which he was grateful for... but the fact she had followed him upset him. All in all, it was a beautiful evening.

He would let her fight her fight, but when the time came, he had some questions for her. As the mace clanged against more makeshift weapons, the comedian gathered

156

his gear, pulled the whetstone from his backpack and began sharpening his blades.

****

Ajax leapt to her feet as the first of the raiders came in her direction. Her cloak billowed behind her as she spun out of the way of the man's spear thrust. His spear was nothing more than a broom handle with a hunting knife attached to the end, but it would do some damage if it found the right spot.

The sound of footsteps alerted her to more foes, and she rushed up the length of the man's spear and drove her mace under his chin. With a crack, his jaw fractured, and when she pulled her mace away, his face sagged where the bones were broken. Inside she grimaced. *That must hurt something fierce.*

With an overhead smash, she put the man out of his misery.

And then she was surrounded by raiders, their skinny arms and legs dancing in the light of the fire. Behind her, a building collapsed in upon itself, sending up another shower of sparks. With extra light to see by, she lashed out at her attackers, breaking one man's wrist so he dropped the metal pipe in his hand. Whirling, she busted the kneecap of another, and his pained scream drowned out the roar of the fire behind her for a moment.

Her strikes were not meant to kill. There were too many of them for that. There were six attackers, and she struggled to keep them at bay. Each blow she struck was meant to disable, as speed was of the utmost importance. The power and force needed for a killing blow would require time, milliseconds maybe, but enough time for one of these men or women to get past her defenses. All she could do was keep moving, lash out when she could, and slowly, she would whittle them down until they were begging for the coup de grace.

A knee here, an elbow, there, her mace stung them all over. They swore and cursed at her, called her names, told her what they were going to do to her body when she was dead. But none of this mattered to her. The snake's hissing wasn't important; it was the bite that had to be avoided.

So far, she had incapacitated two men. One limped along on a shattered kneecap, tears in his eyes, the other swung a sledgehammer at her with his off arm, his strikes as lazy and off-target as a child's. In the midst of the battle, she saw one of her foes step back and look around to find that most of her gang was dead. She took off into the night, beating feet up the fiery path leading through town. *Smart girl.* This left her with four foes to face.

Ajax smiled. She had faced worse odds and won before. The man with the gimpy leg was the first to go. As she swung in a circle, she clocked him across the face. Later, when she would look at their dead bodies, he would look like someone pressing their face up against glass, nose crooked, lips flattened and burst.

That left three. The man with the weak sledgehammer swings and the broken wrist, a woman with a staff, and a fellow with his fists wrapped in barbed wire. They twirled around her, spouting curses, but they would not flee like their smart friend who had already taken off. Their bloodlust was up, and the injured man's eyes dripped with wounded pride.

Three was easy.

She stopped moving, giving her legs a rest, and the man with the barbed-wire fists rushed in at her, delivering a blow to her ribs, the majority of its impact easily deflected by the chainmail underneath her tabard. He looked up at her, surprised to see her lack of a reaction, and she obliterated his face with her mace.

158

She heard the whistle of the staff behind her, so she fell to her knees. The staff hit the pulpy mass of the barbed-wire-fisted man's face. Already gone, the staff's impact sent the man flying to the side where his body began the process of decomposition.

Spinning on her knee, she heard the *thunk* of the one-armed man's sledgehammer as it impacted the dirt. *That was lucky. I'll leave him for last.*

With her plan in place, the Chicken Kicker rose up, waving her mace outwards to deflect the incoming shaft of the woman's staff. Wood clanked off metal, and Ajax gripped the staff in her free hand, the woman jerking and tugging to pull it free. The raider was no match for her strength. Grunting in frustration, the woman dropped her staff and rushed at Ajax, her fists balled. She swung at the Chicken Kicker, who was taller, stronger, and a better fighter. Ajax slapped her hands away like a parent toying with an angry child. Blow after blow the woman threw at her, and Ajax, for a moment, felt as if she was back in the Hall of Justice sparring with Thing, honing her reflexes.

"Arggghhh!" the woman screamed. Her cry was a frustrated primal thing, and Ajax knew she was tired of being toyed with. With a swipe of her mace, she ended the cat and mouse game.

That left the man with the broken wrist. Covered in sweat and grit, he struggled to pull his sledgehammer up and into the air with his one good arm.

Ajax thrust her mace through her belt loop and walked toward the man. As she reached out and placed her hands on the handle of the sledgehammer, the man looked into her eyes. His anger faded. His lips trembled and tears welled in the red-rims of his eyelids. Death was coming, and he knew it. Gently, she pulled the sledgehammer from the man's hands.

"Close your eyes," she said.

The man did as he was told, and Ajax swung the sledgehammer impacting him right in the middle of the chest. He made a gasping sound, and then he flew on his back, his feet flying into the air. His hands searched his chest, probing at the indent where his heart had been turned into pulp. After a few moments, his hands and head fell to the dirt, and all that was left was the comedian.

She turned to look at him, sitting among a field of dead he had planted. He didn't smile at her or acknowledge her in any way. But behind those goggles, she could tell he was studying her.

Chaos and order. This was it. This was what she had been questing for. The man was darkness, and she was light. With the town burning around them, the smell of shit and blood in the air, Ajax stood panting, regaining her breath.

She walked in his direction and then plopped down cross-legged across from him as he dragged a whetstone down the length of his massive sword. The rasping sound put her on edge.

While she regained her strength, she studied the man, that murderous ball of chaos. He hadn't taken a single wound in the battle. His face and goggles were covered in blood, and though he must have fought as hard as she had, he wasn't even sweating or breathing heavily.

This would be an epic fight. She would either go home a hero, or die nameless in the wastes.

Chapter 14: The Broken Man

Ajax, that was her name. She was one of the cleaners. She had followed him across the wastes… and survived. A formidable foe indeed then.

She wanted to kill him; he could sense it. But, as far as he could tell, he had done nothing that would merit her ire. Oh, yeah, he'd killed a load of Fucks, but they had attacked him, so what drove her? He respected a good quest and a good nemesis. Hell, he had his own quest and nemesis to chase. But that was for after.

"You came a long way to find me," he said.

"Indeed."

"You gonna bash me with that mace?"

"Betty willing."

The comedian smirked. So it was true—the Chicken Kickers did worship the Golden Girls. Strange.

He dragged his whetstone down the length of Side-Splitter one last time, and then he placed it back in his backpack amongst all of his other treasures. "If I might ask, why are you so intent on killing me?"

"You are trouble. Wherever you go, people die."

"Maybe it's just that people are dying all over. Correlation doesn't always equal causation."

"I don't know what that means."

The comedian smiled. She was younger than he had expected, although it was hard to tell these days. "Just because someone dies in Shithole, it doesn't necessarily mean I had anything to do with it by being there. Death comes for us all. I just happen to be there sometimes."

"What about the raider you left sitting against the tree?"

The comedian had to think a bit. It had been a while since he had thought about that guy. He had come out of the woods, while he and a wanderer had been sharing a

161

bottle of whiskey the man had found in a wrecked pick-up in the woods. The fire had been burning bright... the whiskey glowed in the firelight, and it went down smooth. At first, he had thought the man with the whiskey had been a raider, intent on taking his goods, but he had just been a stepper, a scavenger who required company more than anything else. A man could go crazy in the wastes; the comedian knew that. It's one of the reasons why he continued to go to towns, though each time he risked his life. If he stayed in the wastes, lived on his own, sooner or later, he would go crazy, and he liked being sane, or on the edge of it anyway.

"I didn't kill that raider," he scoffed.

"Then who did?"

"Some scavver. Me and him were drinking a bottle of whiskey, and this dumbass raider comes running out of the woods, waving his machete in the air."

"But you tied him up with the bungie cord?"

The comedian thought back then. By the time they had finished the bottle of whiskey, they had been wasted. His memories of that were fuzzy, snatches of conversation and laughter in the night, a rarity among the wastes. "I needed an audience."

"For what?"

"My show."

"Your show?"

"My show! What are you deaf? This guy comes out of nowhere, offers me half a bottle of whiskey, the least I could do was repay him with some entertainment."

Ajax scoffed at him. "So you propped him up against the tree, mutilated his body, and did your show."

The comedian shrugged his shoulders. She had the gist of it.

"I think I've heard enough." Ajax stood then, her body backlit by the fire still blazing in the remains of Mitchell.

162

The comedian sighed. He hated what Ajax represented, but he didn't hate her. It would be a shame to kill her. She was a good person after all, just a little misguided. He stood, hefting Side-Splitter in his hands, the tip touching the dirt. Then he waited. He certainly wouldn't be the one who made the first move.

"For order."

The comedian sniggered a bit, but said nothing more.

She drew her mace from her belt loop, and through her shredded shirt, not a tabard, he caught the glimpse of gleaming silver. Not that armor would do any good against Side-Splitter. The weight of the sword, combined with its edge and his own strength, would cut through that chain mail as if it were made of butter. She had to know that.

She inched closer. The comedian's muscles clenched.

Be careful of this one, Oddrey said.

"I know."

Ajax cocked her head to the side. "Know what?"

"Nothing. Come on, come on. I got places to be."

She nodded her head, and then the battle was begun.

Ajax rushed at the comedian, and he stepped to the side to dodge her first blow, dragging his sword behind him. The blade traced a deep furrow in the ground, and he spun with his back to Ajax, presenting her a juicy target. When he spun once more, expecting her to have attacked his unprotected back, she was standing there, out of sword distance. He smiled at her.

See? I told you. She's crafty.

"That she is."

"Who are you talking to?" Ajax asked.

"Talkin' to Odd," he said, keeping it short so he wouldn't lose his concentration.

Then he rushed at her, his knees skidding through the dirt as he leveled a chop at the woman's knees. She

163

hopped over the swing of Side-Splitter, his blade whistling through the space where she had been. Above, in the firelight, he saw the shadow of her mace raised in the air, and he rolled out of the way, as she brought it crashing down into the dirt.

He danced away. He knew about her now. Knew her reflexes, her reach. Oh, sure, he had studied from afar as she had dealt with the last of the raiders, but watching was one thing. Experiencing her cat-like grace was quite another.

As they circled each other, Ajax asked another question. "Who is Odd?"

He glanced down at his chest to indicate the doll head that hung from his jacket pocket. But he was quickly back on guard.

"That doll head is Odd?"

"Well, her full name is Oddrey, but I call her Odd."

"And it talks to you?"

"She. She talks to me. To me, and only me, so don't go gettin' no bright ideas."

The comedian ran at Ajax, and she danced away from his swing, and the next, and the next.

She's fast. I'll give her that.

Without warning, Ajax twirled her mace, whipping raider gore into the dirt, and then she thrust it through her belt loop. "You're insane."

For some reason, these words angered the comedian, and he rushed at her, swinging Side-Splitter from side to side, twirling into an overhand chop and then bringing his blade up in a half-moon on the backswing. Ajax dodged all of these attacks, but still the comedian's rage grew.

Ajax backed away, dodging chops, stabs, and swings effortlessly. It was easy to do when you didn't plan on fighting back.

"Come on, come on. Let's finish this!" the comedian called, frustration edging into his voice.

Instead of fighting back, Ajax did the strangest thing. She stepped back, bowed deeply at him and then knelt on one knee. She placed her hands on her elevated knee, crossing them. Her pale skin glowed orange in the firelight.

It's a trick, Oddrey said.

"I know that. I know it," he grunted.

The comedian shook his head. This was the oddest fight he had ever been a part of. He raised Side-Splitter into the air half-heartedly, but Ajax made no move to defend herself. "What the fuck are you doing? Aren't you going to fight?"

"I cannot kill the crazed, for they are sick and in need of healing."

"I'm not crazy, well, maybe like a fox, but not like a gibber-man."

"You're talking to a doll head for Sophia's sake."

"She's not a doll head," the comedian stammered. Somewhere in his brain, strange things were happening. Things he didn't like. *Ajax... she's the cause of this.*

Kill her, Odd said. *Be done with her.*

The comedian raised his hands over his head, held his sword the way Conan would have, and then he brought it down. The blade bit the dust, sinking into the dry soil of Mitchell.

When he opened his eyes, he found himself staring into the jade eyes of Ajax, their green color augmented in the firelight by the black and red face paint running across her face in matching horizontal stripes.

"Fight, damn you."

"You are the Broken Man. To kill you would be a crime against order."

"I'll break you!"

"No, you won't."

165

The comedian stood then, pulling his blade behind him. He walked and sat in the dirt. A deep sigh escaped him. "I'm tired."

"It's exhausting to be broken."

"Would you stop saying that?"

Ajax shrugged, and sat there, quiet and studying.

Then he laughed, like the madman she thought he was.

"What are you laughing at?"

"You. You come all this way to kill me, and then you don't. There's a joke in there somewhere."

"I doubt you could find it."

The comedian, his ire fading, leaned back on his elbows. The day had been long, and the warmth of a burning town warmed him as the sweat cooled on his body. "I need to sleep," he said suddenly.

"Do as you must."

"Well, why don't you sleep over there," he said, pointing in a random direction.

"Oh, no. I can't do that."

The comedian grunted. "Why not?"

"I mean to heal you."

"Because I'm *broken*?" He punctuated the words with air quotes.

Ajax nodded.

"You snore?"

"Not that I know of?"

"Good."

With that, the comedian rolled over on his side, grumbling to himself and to Odd in near-silent whispers. "Goddamn weirdo thinks I'm broken. She's the one with the brokenness."

She wants to help you.

"Well, I say she can fuck right off. I don't need some Chicken Kicker following me around, looking over my shoulder every time I need to defend myself."

It could be nice to have some company.

"I don't want company. I got you—and why didn't you say anything? She thinks I'm crazy now."

You are crazy.

"Like a fox," they both said together. With that, the comedian closed his eyes and went to the land of sleep, where the past became real, and his body and memory still existed as one. He was not a broken man there, but he always wished he was.

****

Ajax studied the comedian in his sleep. She could have killed him, maybe. The way he twitched and jerked when he slept concerned her. He mumbled, his fists clenching and unclenching in the darkness.

Ajax turned away from the strange man and watched as the town burned. She pulled one of Beandick's pomatoes from her bag and gnawed on it as the words of The Fury glowed in her mind.

"Beware the Broken Man, for he has the power to change this world, for better or worse."

Prophecy, spiritualism. She had always hated these things. As far as she was concerned, it was just a bunch of nonsense. But here he was—the Broken Man, and he was just about as broken as a man could be. Why, he was little more than a mad dog when it came down to it.

But if he could be fixed, they could fix the world, according to the prophecy. Of course, this could all be a huge mistake, and he might just be a crazy waster, nothing more. Maybe she was reading more into this situation than she should. Well, she had made mistakes before. She would follow him until she could be sure.

She spit the seeds of the pomato into the dirt. She didn't much care for them. But the flesh was alright. After she ate, she took one last look at the comedian, jerking and twitching in his sleep like a tortured thing, and then she

167

turned in. The smell of smoke and blood wafted over the pair, bathing them in the new fragrance of the earth.

Epilogue: The Glow Crone's Prophecy

The next day was one long silent walk. The comedian seemed to trudge onward without a care in the world. He didn't speak, not even to his doll head. He refused to acknowledge the presence of Ajax, and they strode in silence, scanning the skies and the waste fog for signs of trouble, but for a wonder, none presented themselves.

As they walked, the fog began to thin, and they knew they were coming to a place, perhaps the place the comedian was searching for.

At the end of their day, they sat on the dusty ground, dragged a handful of desiccated logs into a pile and lit a fire. As the chill of the wastes settled over the land, they sat staring into the fire, the comedian ignoring Ajax, and Ajax trying to find some way to get the comedian to accept her.

They sat like that for a long time, staring into the flames. Time passed until the flames turned to coals. They enjoyed the feeling of warmth as the logs returned to the earth and the sky, embers dancing among the shifting radiator-fluid-colored lights in the atmosphere.

The comedian stared into the sky, trying to understand the meaning of it all and having no luck, when an old woman appeared out of the waste fog, glowing faintly.

"Stay back," he said to the woman. She carried in her hand a stout stick and walked in a robe that was mostly tatters. It had once been white, but now it was as grey as the waste fog.

The woman held her distance, eyeing the fire longingly. Her face was long, her nose beaked, and her skin cracked in thousands upon thousands of wrinkles. A person could get lost tracing all the cracks on the woman's face.

"Please. I only long for warmth. The nights are ever so cold."

Ajax and the comedian shared a glance.

"What are you doing out here?" Ajax asked, as suspicious as the comedian.

"I have the glow."

"Well, I don't want the fucking glow," the comedian said. "Buzz off."

"It's not contagious. No one in the towns will listen though. Please, I have things I can offer."

The comedian's mind, frequently in the gutter, said, "I don't want anything you have to offer."

The woman, glowing in the night, her stick-thin arms trembling, begged this time. "Oh, please, oh, please. I'll freeze out here. I've been cold for so long. Please let me sit by your fire. I can tell your future. The glow has taken much from me, but it offers its gifts as well."

"A glow crone," Ajax whispered.

"What the fuck is a glow crone?"

"People say that sometimes, a person affected with the glow can tell the future."

The comedian said nothing. His first instinct was to tell her to fuck off, but the night was unusually cold. As far as the future went, he wanted no part of it. "You can sit, but if you do, sit quietly and stay away from me."

The old woman smiled, embarrassed by her neediness, as she sat cross-legged across the fire from him.

"Whoa, whoa. Cover that up," the comedian said.

The woman adjusted her tatters and apologized profusely. "Used to be that men wanted it all the time, but not anymore," she said.

They fell into a deep silence, the fire sputtering and consuming the wood.

"Would you like your future told?"

170

"No," the comedian said, flat as a dime.

"I would," Ajax said. She had always held a fascination with the holy folks, the people who could see a world that existed beyond the grit, sweat, and blood of the mundane world.

The glow crone nodded and said, "Your future is his future. Without him, you are nothing, so, if I am to tell you about your path, I need tell you of his path as well. Will you allow it?" This last she directed at the comedian.

"I'm going to bed. Do what you want."

The comedian rolled onto his side then, and the glow crone spoke, her voice dragging out of her throat like nails on a chalkboard. "The world grows weary, the sun dies, the earth cracks like an old person's hand in the chill of winter. This you know."

Shut up. Shut up. Shut up. The comedian wished he had something to block out the voice of the glow crone. At this point, he would take the cries of a shrieker.

"That which is broken must be mended. Trust the bones to knit together on their own. Once they are set, they will grow back together. Make a splint of those who need him. Use them to bind the broken, for in each of them is the material required to make him whole. And when he is whole, the world will be whole, but if he should break, if you should lose hope, the world will die, you, him, all of us. Except for Canada. Canada is going to be fine."

Nonsense. What utter nonsense.

"The way is not easy, the people you meet will not be either. Your path is a circle, and some things that have been, will not be again. Let it not break you, for if you break, so too will the broken. A thing may mend if care is taken, but if you are reckless, that thing may be broken beyond repair. Your lucky numbers are 2, 4, and 20."

"Is that it?" Ajax asked.

"What do you mean is that it? That's pretty fucking good if you ask me. Young people, always asking for gifts

171

and favors and then spitting in your face when you give them what they want. What else could you want to know? I told you about the fate of the world. Is there something bigger than that?"

Ajax fell silent, and the comedian waited to hear her answer, but none was forthcoming.

"Oh, I see. A romantic," the crone said. She cackled, and lights flashed on the inside of his eyelids as if his brain itself desired not to hear her voice anymore.

"Love came once for you, and it would have been pure as pre-war snow. But that was the one shot you had. All loves from henceforth shall be work, shall be give and take, hate and love, equal parts struggle and success. Love comes but once for each of us, and when it is gone, it is gone for good."

The comedian harrumphed in his head. He could have told Ajax that.

The group lapsed into silence, and overhead, ancient satellites, their purposes long forgotten, entered the atmosphere, burning up in the sky, shooting stars that could have once been seen by billions, now only witnessed by a handful of people who bothered to look up from the dusty ground that could open up at a moment's notice and swallow them whole.

"Good night, Odd," he whispered, the crone's words fading in his ears.

Goodnight, Broken Man.

"Not you too," he grumbled.

Ajax heard the words and knew the comedian talked to the doll hanging on his chest. She smiled apologetically at the crone, and they both lay down, letting the heat of the fire keep the chill of the wastes at bay. The crone's words rattled around in Ajax's head, and she dreamed of Kevin Fever, wondering just how accurate the crone's words were. She hoped the glow crone was wrong about everything, but as is the way with most fortune tellers, she told enough of

172

the truth and mixed it with enough mystery to make Ajax's mind whirl.

Little did Ajax know the crone had told the same spiel to dozens of travelers kind enough to let her share their fire over the years. It was a good spiel that got the job done.

A Word From Jacy

Thank you for reading *One Night Stand in the Wastes*! I hope you've been enjoying the comedian's crazy adventures. If you have, please leave a review! As an indie author, the only marketing I receive is from fellow readers like you!

If you enjoyed One Night Stand at the End of the World, check out the third book, One Night Stand in Ike! The comedian's journey continues! Watch as he encounters strange characters, strange lands, and his own strange mind. The comedian's journey will continue. Right now, I'm not sure how many books will be in the series, but if it goes on forever, I wouldn't mind, as I have so much fun writing them! In the meantime, I'll be working on the next installment!

One Night Stand in Ike is available on amazon!

Get Free Stuff from Jacy Morris

Building a relationship with my readers is super important to me. Please join my newsletter for information on new books and deals plus all this free content:

1. A free copy of This Rotten World: Part One.

2. A free copy of The Lady That Stayed, a horror novella inspired by real life.

3. A free copy of The Pied Piper of Hamelin, a twisted fairy tale like nothing you've ever seen before.

You can get your content for free, by signing up at https://landingpage.jacymorris.com/home-copy-1

Also By Jacy Morris

In the One Night Stand Series

One Night Stand at the End of the World

The world is gone, and it's not coming back. The rules have changed, but one man refuses to lay down and die. A comedian, shattered and broken, wanders the wasteland on a quest that only he knows and understands. Zombies, raiders, talking doll heads, shady merchants and unbeatable gamblers all stand in the way of The Comedian's success, but through the power of comedy, he will find a way.

Available on amazon!

One Night Stand in the Wastes

Book two in the One Night Stand series. With his sights set on a mysterious place named Ike, the comedian journeys across a shattered and broken wasteland, confronting demons both inner and outer. Behind him, justice dogs his footsteps in the form of Ajax, a ruthless arbiter of order who is hellbent on ending the comedian's chaotic ways. Killer squirrels, mutated humans, and raiders galore await the comedian in the blasted lands.

Available on amazon!

One Night Stand in Ike

Book three in the One Night Stand series. After journeying across the wastes, the comedian and his companion finally make their way to the town of Ike. There they find a twisted world based upon the rules of corporate society. In order for the comedian to complete his quest, the pair of survivors must play by the rules of Ike's regional manager... or they could, you know, kill everyone. We'll see.

Available on amazon!

In the This Rotten World Series

This Rotten World

A sickness runs rampant through the world. In Portland, Oregon it is no different. As the night takes hold, eight men and women bear witness to the horror of a zombie outbreak. This Rotten World is the zombie novel that horror fans have been waiting for. Where other zombie works skip over the best part of a zombie outbreak, This Rotten World revels in it the downfall of humanity, dragging you through the beginnings of society's death, kicking and screaming.

Available on amazon!

This Rotten World: Let It Burn

It didn't take long for Portland, Oregon to fall. Amid a decaying and crumbling city, a group of survivors hides amid the smoke and the fire. They need to get out of the city... which is easier said than done with thousands of zombies blocking the path. Witness the terrifying flight of these survivors as they leave the city behind and Let It Burn.

Available on amazon!

This Rotten World: No More Heroes

With the smoking ruins of Portland behind them, our survivors find that they have a new enemy to contend with... other survivors. With the dead hounding them at every step and humanity struggling to hold onto its civility, the survivors face their greatest challenge yet. At the end of this battle, there will be No More Heroes.

Available on amazon!

This Rotten World: Winter of Blood

Winter falls hard on Oregon, burying the world under snow and ice. One group of survivors, stuck in a tomb of their own creation, fights to survive, while another group treks across the snowbound countryside, leaving a trail of bloody footprints in their wake... and an army of the undead. The Pacific Ocean calls. Safety calls. But as Mother Nature rakes her frozen claws across the land, the coast could hardly seem further away. Will our survivors make it through this Winter of Blood, or will they be buried by an avalanche of the dead? Find out in the thrilling 4th installment of This Rotten World... This Rotten World: Winter of Blood.

Available on amazon!

This Rotten World: Choking on the Ashes

As our survivors near the coast, the road takes its toll. Falling apart physically and emotionally, they are drawn to the siren call of the beach. Seaside awaits them, a town demolished by a tsunami and crawling with the reanimated. With infants in tow, the survivors must band together to fight for a new home. All that stands between them and the future is an army of the dead. Will they succeed, or will they find themselves Choking on the Ashes?

Available on amazon!

This Rotten World: Rally and Rot

Introducing an entirely new cast of characters, Rally and Rot continues This Rotten World's tradition of zombie excellence. Every summer, Monktree, Wyoming holds a biker rally, an underground event policed by the bikers themselves. When a tragic accident kicks off the zombie apocalypse, the survivors must band together to make it out of town.

Available on amazon!

In the Enemies of Our Ancestors Series

The Enemies of Our Ancestors

In the mountains of the Southwest, in the time before the continents were known, the future of the entire world rested upon the shoulders of a boy prophet whose abduction would threaten to break the world. As a youth, Kochen witnessed the death of his father at the hands of a gruesome spirit that stalked his village's farmlands. From that moment forth, he became a ward of the priests of the village in the cliffs. As he grew, he would begin to experience horrific visions, gifts from the spirits, that all of the other priests dismissed. When the ancient enemies of the Cliff People raid the village and steal Kochen away, they set in motion world-changing events, which threaten to break the shackles that bind the spirits to the earth. A group of hunters are sent to bring Kochen back to his rightful place. As Kochen's power grows, so too does the power of the spirits, and with the help of an ancient seer and his hunter allies, he seeks to restore balance to the world as it falls into brutal madness.

Available on amazon!

The Enemies of Our Ancestors: The Cult of the Skull

With the world balanced after the tragedies of the year before, two tribes attempt to come together and form a whole. But as an ancient foe from the past reappears and a new threat from the south snakes its way to them, the Stick People and the Cliff People must do more than put their differences aside... they must come together to survive. As fantastic as it is violent, The Cult of the Skull picks up right where The Enemies of Our Ancestors left off.

Available on amazon!

The Enemies of Our Ancestors: Broken Spirits

Time has passed. The children of the tribes have grown. Peace has reigned as three tribes have tried to learn to live together. But now, an old terror rears its head. Together, the three tribes will have to learn to fight as one. The thrilling conclusion to The Enemies of Our Ancestors series.

Available on amazon!

Standalone Novels

The Abbey

In the desolate mountains of Scotland, there is an abbey that time has forgotten. Its buildings have crumbled, and the monks that once lived there, guarding the abbey's secret, are long dead. When the journal of a crazed monk is discovered, so is the secret of Inchorgrath Abbey. There are tunnels underneath the abbey and in them resides a secret long forgotten. Together with a group of mercenaries, her would-be boyfriend, and her cutthroat professor, Lasha Arkeketa will travel across the world to uncover the secret of The Abbey.

Available on amazon!

The Drop

How many hearts can a song touch? How many ears can it reach? How many people can it kill? When popular boy band Whoa-Town releases their latest album, no one thinks anything of it. They certainly don't think that the world will be changed forever. After an apocalyptic disease sweeps the world, it becomes clear that the music of this seemingly innocuous boy band had something to do with it, but how? Katherine Maddox, her life irrevocably changed by a disease dubbed The Drop, sets out to find out how and why, to prevent something like The Drop from ever happening again.

Available on amazon!

The Pied Piper of Hamelin

A sickness has come to the village of Hamelin. Born on the backs of rats, a plague begins to spread. As the town rips itself apart, a stranger appears to offer them salvation. But when the citizens of the town fail to hold up their end of the bargain, the stranger returns and exacts a toll that is still spoken of to this day. That toll? The town's entire population of children. This is the legend of the Pied Piper. It is no fairy tale. It is a nightmare. Are you prepared to hear his song?

Available on amazon!

Killing the Cult

At any one time, there are 4,000 cults operating within the United States. In Logansport, Indiana, one cult is growing. When The Benevolent recruit Matt Rust's estranged daughter, he journeys to their compound to free her, one way or another. Unfortunately, for Matt Rust, his checkered past threatens to derail his rescue mission. When word gets out that Rust has reemerged after spending the last decade in the witness protection program, drug tzar Emilio Cartagena sends his best men after Rust. Will he be able to save his daughter before Cartagena's men arrive? Find out as Matt Rust tries Killing the Cult.

Available on amazon!

The Lady That Stayed

Land has a price. It's always been that way. When J.S. Stensrud and his wife Dotty buy a piece of land on the Oregon coast known as the Spit, they come to know that price. As Stensrud tries to build a legacy on his island amid the background of the Great Depression, he is visited by a Native American woman who helps him learn the bloody price of land in the most painful way possible.

Available on amazon!

The Taxidermied Man

Bud got stuffed, and now he has a front row seat to the downfall of man.

Suffering from early-onset dementia due to alcoholism, Bud wants nothing more than to be there for his wife forever—so he has his body stuffed. Unfortunately, his wife is not at all pleased, and after she dies, Bud is sold off to the highest bidder only to be used as a sex toy, a sports trophy, and finally a God. As his imprisoned mind unravels, Bud witnesses the collapse of humanity through static eyes and an unchanging body.

Available on amazon!

An Unorthodox Cure

Cancer will touch all of our lives at one point or another. It may affect someone you know, someone you respect, or even someone you love. In the case of the Cutters, it has systematically invaded every cell of their daughter's body. When the doctors admit there is nothing they can do, the Cutters bring their daughter home and prepare to wait for the inevitable. Just as they accept defeat, a mysterious doctor appears at their door, offering a miraculous cure and kindling hope in their hearts. The only catch? The Cutters have to decide what is more important, their daughter's life or her soul.

Available on amazon!

About the Author

Jacy Morris is a Native American author who has brought to life zombies, cults, demons, killer boy bands, and spirits. You can learn more about him at the following:

Website: http://jacymorris.com

Email: jacy@jacymorris.com

Facebook:
https://www.facebook.com/JacyMorrisAuthor/

Twitter: https://twitter.com/Vocabulariast

Be sure to check out

THE

DROP

By Jacy Morris

Here is a sneak preview:

PROLOGUE

An excerpt from an article entitled "Whoa-Town Becoming Whoa-World in Record Time" by Anton Russo as Published in *Rolling Stone*

Part of me wants to hate them. Boy bands aren't supposed to be this good. A man, a grown-ass, thirty-year-old man, shouldn't find himself moved by the vocal-stylings of five boys, some not even old enough to drink yet. But here I am, at Wembley Stadium, packed in like cattle in a slaughterhouse chute, ready to stick my head into the kill box and have a hole punched in my cranium.

There is no opening band for Whoa-Town. What sucker would take that gig? Who would want to have the memory of their performance obliterated by the next act, a band that many claim is bigger than the Beatles and the Stones combined? Lofty words. All of us scoffing, bearded, music snobs sneer, knowing full well in our hearts that there is no way anyone means it when they throw out those comparisons. It's just the thing that clichéd, hack journalists say when they can't think of any way of telling people how big a band is or is going to be.

Here I am, standing amid the heat and the hot breath of 90,000 people, the lucky ones who snagged their tickets in that first two minutes before the entire system crashed. Leading to a day in London collectively known as Cry Day, the day that every teenage girl, and many other men, women, and boys christened their cell phones with tears at news that the Whoa-Town show was already sold out.

You'd expect the air to reek of cheap designer-knockoff perfume, hair product and bubblegum. But it doesn't. It smells of something else. It reeks instead of lust and anticipation. The crowd hums with energy; their faces drip sweat even though the stadium's roof is open to the elements. The cool night air can't compete with their fever. Their bodies vibrate, conducting heat at a level that confirms in my mind that spontaneous combustion might actually be a thing. At any moment, the girl next to me, screaming ear-piercing "woos" every thirty seconds or so, might burst into flames.

Before long, we can't take it anymore. Wait... they can't take it. I'm certainly not into any boy band. I'm just here for the story. They begin to chant. When the mother next to me, clad in baggy jeans that go up past her bellybutton, elbows me as encouragement, I make a show of reluctantly joining in. I clap. I yell, "Whoa-Town!" right along with everyone else.

Only when the building quakes from all the stomping, yelling, and clapping does something happen. Just as I am assured that Wembley Stadium will collapse around us before the band ever takes stage, the lights come on, blinding us. The lights fade, dropping faster than my own aloof persona, plunging us into a darkness punctuated by the unwelcome glow of emergency lighting. Around the stadium, tiny rectangular blooms of blue-light illuminate in response. 90,000 people recording when they aren't supposed to be. It is as if the stadium is filled with thousands of mutant fireflies, swaying from side to side as the chant of "Whoa-Town!" thunders through the stadium once again... and then the beat drops.

With a "whoomp," several sparking shapes arc into the air, erupting into gold and crimson starbursts, and screams echo so loudly that I'm not even sure when the *screaming stops and the music begins. They're here. Whoa-Town, the boys that will change music and the world forever and I, Anton Russo, was there.*

Tragic. Just tragic. - Sebastian

You think that's tragic, check out those *Teen Beat* articles I found. - Katherine

Chapter 1: Walking the Streets

I see this story as more than a job, more than just a fact-finding mission to once again help us cope with the tragedy, with a loss that, in a very real sense, is unprecedented. Many people have tried that. So many. No, if that's all this was, then I would be off somewhere else, looking into a murder or trying to uncover the next dastardly person exploiting the American Relief Organization.

I see this story as a time capsule, a way to help the people of the future. If there's one thing that I learned from my 8th-grade social studies teacher, it's that history is a cycle, and that all things, good or bad, will come around again, hence the term revolution, a circuit, a never-ending loop that only the educated can see. Thinking about what the world has just gone through, and is still going through, I can only shudder at the thought that hundreds of years down the line this will all happen again. So my hope is to write this story, bury it in the ground, and when it's needed, the people of the future can come and dig it up.

People will need to know, not so much the people that are still alive, but the people of the future. The people still alive already know about The Drop. They're so tired of thinking about it that they don't actually want to know the truth of the situation. They can't help but see The Drop around them. Examining it further is just poking at a poorly stitched together wound with a razorblade. Sooner or later it's going to open up. Sooner or later, it's going to bleed. They don't want to know how the knife that stabbed them in the chest was forged. They don't want to know where the steel came from, how the ivory handle was carved from the tusk of a poached elephant. None of that will help them.

But for the people of the future, that's a different story altogether. The Drop was our Black Plague, and just as our knowledge of the spread of the plague prevents it from happening again, this article is vital to preventing another Drop.

I'm in the Big Apple. They call it the Big Rotten Core now. As I walk down Broadway, I'm struck by its similarity to the post-apocalyptic movies I over-consumed as a teenager. The emptiness of the streets, very *I Am Legend.* The newspaper tumbling through the intersection, unchecked like a tumbleweed through a western town, very *The Road.* The sad motherfucker leaning up against the wall, smoking a cigarette, and staring at the cracked and crumbling concrete, very *Book of Eli.*

The street ends at Times Square, once a mega-hub of awesomeness where cowboys played guitar in their underwear and an unceasing cavalcade of electric, sex-themed ads assaulted wayward tourists. It was now just a scene from *The Postman.* There weren't enough people to provide upkeep for the cities. Those that stayed did so because they had become ghosts themselves, haunted by the losses of The Drop. They stuck around, though no more food was coming, except for that which they grew themselves. Though the children didn't play hopscotch on the streets and the stoplights had been turned off, the ghosts remained, remembering the glory of New York and its eight-and-a-half-million residents.

Glass crunches under my boots as I turn and look inside the Disney Store... all those toys just sitting there, no one left to play with them. I step inside. The cash register was busted open a long time ago, but the toys sit waiting. And I can't help but wonder who will actually benefit from the story that I am going to tell.

The next generation, I suppose, the ones that will grow up without music. The ones that will grow up without the internet, they'll want these dolls. They'll want something to play with.

I exit the Disney Store, sick of looking at clownish, Dory plush dolls. I am in time for the show. The man at the end of the street puts a gun in his mouth and pulls the trigger. Blood sprays the wall behind him. I scream like a maniac, but somehow, no one in Times Square hears me... because I'm the only person left alive in a place that was once called "The Crossroads of the World." And I wonder, was that man just waiting for someone to stumble along? Was he waiting for an audience before he killed himself? Or were his sixty days up?

I shudder and call the police. "Hello?... Yeah, there's been a suicide in Times Square... What do you mean three hours?"

I hang up. I go back inside the Disney store, and I grab myself a Dory plushy, and I hold onto it for dear life as the man's blood and brains run down the wall. This was probably the worst vacation idea I had ever had.

Available on amazon!

Be sure to check out

The Abbey

By Jacy Morris

Here is a sneak preview:

THE ABBEY

PROLOGUE

He would make him scream. So far they had all screamed, their unused voices quaking and cracking with pain that was made even worse by the fact that they were breaking their vows to their Lord, their sole reason for existence. Shattering their vows was their last act on earth, and then they were gone. Now there was only one left. A lone monk had taken flight into the abbey's lower regions, a labyrinthine winding of corridors and catacombs lined with the boxed up remains of the dead and their trinkets.

Brenley Denman's boots clanked off of the rough-hewn, blue stone as he trounced through the abbey's crypts, following the whiff of smoke from the monk's torch and the echo of his harried footsteps. His men were spread out through the underworks, funneling the monk ahead of them, driving him the way hounds drove a fox. The monk would lead them to his den, and then the prize would be theirs. And then the world.

He held his torch up high, watching the flames glimmer off of golden urns and silver swords, ancient relics of a nobility that had long since gone extinct, their glory only known by faded etchings in marble sarcophagi, the remaining glint of their once-prized possessions, and the spiders who built their webs in the darkness. Once they were done with the monk, they would take anything that glittered, but first they needed the talisman, the fabled bauble that resided at the bottom of the mountain the abbey was built on.

Throughout the land, legends of the talisman had been told for decades around hearthfires and inns throughout the isles. Then the tellers had begun to vanish, until the talisman of Inchorgrath and its stories had all but been forgotten. But Denman knew. He remembered the stories his father had told him while they sat around the fire of their stone house, built less than ten yards from the cemetery. His father's knuckles were cracked and dried from hours in the elements digging graves and rifling pockets when no one was looking. He knew secrets when he saw them. His father had first heard the story from the old Celts, the remains of the land's indigenous population, reduced to poverty and begging in the streets. His father said the old Celts' stories were two-thirds bullshit and one-third truth. They told of a relic, a key to the Celts' uprising and reclamation of the land, buried in the deepest part of the tallest mountain on the Isles. Of course, they spoke of regeneration and the return of Gods among men as well, but the relic... that was the important part. That was the part that was worth money. And now, he was here, with his men, ready to make his fortune.

He heard shouts, but it was impossible to tell where they were coming from. Sound echoed and bounced off of the blue, quartzite stone blocks, warping reality. He chose the corridor to his right, quickening his pace, his long legs eating up the distance. His men knew not to start without him, but you never knew when a monk would lash out, going against their discipline and training and earning a sword through the throat for their duplicity. That would be unacceptable to Denman. The monk must scream before he died.

His breathing quickened along with his pace, and he could feel the warmth of anticipation spread through his limbs as his breath puffed into the cold crypt air. Miles... they had come miles through these crypts, twisting and turning, burrowing into the secret heart of the earth, chasing the last monk who skittered through the hallways like a spider. The other monks had all known the secret of the abbey, the power it harbored, the relic it hid in its bowels. To a man, they had sat on their knees, their robes collecting condensation in the green grass of the morning, refusing to divulge the abbey's mysteries.

They had died, twisted, mangled and beaten. But still, all he could pull from them were the screams, musical expulsions of the throat that he ended with a smile as he dragged the razor-fine edge of his knife across their throats. Their blood had bubbled out, vivid against the morning sun, to splash on the grass.

When there was only one left, they had let him go. The youngest monk in the abbey, grown to manhood, but still soft about the face, his intelligent eyes filled with horror, stood and ran, his robe stained with the pooled blood of the monks that had died to his left and right. He was like one of the homing pigeons they used in the lowlands, leading them to home... to the relic. They had chased him, hooting and hollering the whole way, their voices and taunts driving the monk before them like a fox. The chase would end at his burrow; it always did.

Ahead, he heard laughing, and with that Denman knew that the chase was at an end. He rounded one last corner to see the monk being worked over by his men, savage pieces of stupidity who were good for two things, lifting heavy objects and killing people. Denman waved his hand and they let the suffering monk go. The monk sagged to the ground, his head bent over, his eyes leaking tears. He sobbed in silence.

Denman stood in the secret of the crypt, a room at the heart of the mountain, the place where legends hid. How deep had they gone? At first there had been stairs, but then they had reached a deeper part of the crypt where the corridors twisted and turned, the floor pitched ever downward. Time and distance had lost all meaning in the breast of the world. How long had it taken them to carve this place, the monks working in silence to protect their treasure? Hundreds of years? A thousand?

The room was simple and small, as the order's aesthetics demanded, filled by Denman and the nine men that he had brought to take the abbey's secrets. Wait, one was missing. He looked at his men, brutal pieces of humanity, covered in dirt, mud and blood. The boy wasn't there. Denman shrugged. He would find his way down eventually.

The walls of the room were blue-gray, stone blocks stacked one on top of the other without the benefit of mortar, the weight of the mountain providing the only glue that was needed. The only other features of the room were an alcove with two thick, tallow candles in cheap tin holders and an ancient oak table.

The smoke from his men's torches hung in the air, creating a stinging miasma that stung his eyes. Brenley Denman squatted next to the monk and used his weathered hand to raise the monk's head by his chin. He looked into the monk's eyes, and instead of the fear that he expected to see, there was something else.

"What is this? Defiance?" he asked, amused by the monk's bravado. Denman stood and kicked the monk in the mouth with his boot, a shit-covered piece of leather that was harder than his heart; teeth and blood decorated the stones.

"Where is it?" he asked the monk. There was no answer. Denman had expected none. Say what you will about the Lord's terrestrial servants, but they were loyal... which made everything more difficult... more exhilarating. Denman was a man that loved a challenge.

He handed his torch to one of his men, a broken-faced simpleton whose only gifts were strength and the ability to do what he was told. Denman knew that he would need both hands to make the monk sing his secrets.

"Hand me the Tearmaker," he said to another of his men. Radan, built like a rat with stubby arms and powerful legs, reached to his belt and produced a knife, skinny and flexible, designed not so much for murder as it was for removing savory meat from skin and fat. It made excellent work of fish, and it would most likely prove delightfully deft at making a tight-lipped monk break his vows.

As he reached out to take the proffered knife from his man, the monk scrambled to his feet and dove for the alcove. Before they could stop him, the monk grasped both of the candle sticks and yanked on them. The candlesticks rose into the air. Rusted, metal chains were affixed to their bases, and they clanked against the surrounding stone of the alcove as the monk pulled on them.

The distant sound of stones grinding upon stones reverberated throughout the crypt. Somewhere, something was moving. Denman glared at the monk. The robed figure dropped the candlesticks and turned to face them. With his head cast downward, he reached into the folds of his robe and produced a rosary. He folded his hands and began to

197

pray, beads moving through his fingers, his lips moving without making sound.

The crypt shook as an unseen weight clattered through the halls of the crypt. Dust fell from the ceiling, hanging in the air, buoyed upwards by the tumbling smoke of their torches.

"What have you done?" Denman asked.

The monk did not respond. Instead, he reached into the hanging sleeve of one of his robes and produced a small stone thimble, roughly-made and ancient. It was shiny and black, the type of black that seemed to steal the light from the room. The monk put it up to his mouth, hesitated for a second and then swallowed it, grimacing in pain as the object slid down his throat.

In the hallway behind them, the grinding had stopped. The crypt was silent, but for the guttering of the torches and their own breathing. "Go see what happened," he said to the oaf and the rat. The other men followed them, leaving Denman alone with the monk and his unceasing, silent supplications to the Lord above.

Denman forced the monk onto the oak table. He offered little resistance. With Tearmaker in his hand, Denman began to carve the skin lovingly off of the monk's fingers. First, he carved a circle around the man's fingers, then a line. With the edge of his knife, he prodded a corner of the skin up, and then, grasping tightly, he ripped the skin away from the muscle and bone, dropping the wet flesh onto the ground. He did this to each finger, one by one. Sweat stood out on Denman's brow, and the monk had yet to scream. He hadn't so much as gasped or hissed in pain. He was turning out to be more work than he was worth.

Except for the blood pulsing from his skinned fingers, he appeared to be asleep, his eyes softly closed.

"Where is it, you bastard?" There was no response but for the bleeding.

Denman pulled the monk's robe up around his waist. It was a quick jump, but he was eager to be done with the man on the table. Usually, he would take his time with a challenge like the monk, savoring the sensation of skin ripping from muscle and bone, but he could feel the weight of the mountain about him, its walls shrinking with every minute. Sweat covered his body, and the monk's calm demeanor was unnerving.

Radan rounded the corner at a run, his body dripping with sweat and panic on his face. He skidded to a stop, his boots grinding dust into the blue stones. "We're sealed in here," he said.

Denman looked at the monk lying on the table. His hand gripped Tearmaker tight. "What have you done?" The monk lay there, his eyes closed, a look of peace on his face. "What have you done!" he screamed, jabbing the knife into the monk's ribs. Then Denman saw the monk's hands. Where before his index and pointer finger had been reduced to skinless chunks of muscle and bone dripping blood on the table, there was now skin. "Impossible," Denman whispered.

The monk's eyes snapped open, and finally, Denman got the scream that he had been waiting for.

Available on amazon!

Be sure to check out

THE PIED

PIPER

OF HAMELIN

By Jacy Morris

Here is a sneak preview:

The Pied Piper of Hamelin

Prologue: The River Weser

The boat captain sailed down the river, the wind ruffling his long, salt-and-pepper locks. It was a fine day. His ship was laden with goods, and he was relishing the prospect of turning a nice profit for himself and his crew. He should have been happy, ecstatic, singing shanties that would turn a barmaid's face red, but he wasn't.

The captain sniffed inward, pulling a grimy film of mucus into the back of his throat. He hacked up a thick glob and deposited it into the Weser River. He could taste the blood in it. His men were no better. Though they were ill, they still did their jobs. After all, a boatswain who couldn't earn his keep wouldn't receive his full share. On top of that, as an example to his men, the captain continued to work, stalking the decks and shouting out orders, though all he wanted to do was go down below and curl up in his cabin. He felt as if his head was trying to split in half, and he had an uncomfortable swelling in his groin that sent sharp pains through his entire body every time he moved.

Out of the corner of his eye, he spied furtive movement. Goddamn rats, he thought to himself. He would have to see if he could find some sort of boat cat in the next town. He consulted his charts, hand-drawn, passed down from captain to captain, and saw that the next village would be Hamelin.

It was an uppity berg; the mayor was trying to turn it into Rome from what the goodfolk at the pier told him.

They had no need of Rome in this part of the world. What they needed was good strong ale, women with weak morals, and more good strong ale. Or maybe that's just what he needed.

A chilly breeze washed over the river, and the captain pulled his jacket tighter, gritting his teeth at the sharp pain the movement caused him. Underneath his arms, there were more swellings, unnatural lumps that seemed as if they were nothing but bundles of nerves. Pulling the jacket tighter had been like jabbing a flame-heated knife, point first, into each of his armpits.

Without warning, he began to cough like he had never coughed before. Black spots swam in front of his eyes, and for a brief moment, he thought, This is it. This is how I die. But then the coughing passed, and he was able to grab a raspy breath of air. The muscles in his back felt worse for wear, and he spat a wad of red-flecked phlegm into the river.

The breeze kicked up again, but this time, he didn't bother to readjust his jacket. Instead, he let the wind wash over him, evaporating the fever sweat from his brow.

"Captain," his first mate said, "Old Gert is dead."

It took a while for the words to sink into his fever-addled mind, but when they did, he did the only thing he could do. "Pitch him over the side, lad. It's a water-burial for him."

Normally, they would keep the body in the cold hull of the ship so that his family could bury him proper, but with all of the rats on board, it would be more dignified to give him to the river than to let those furry bastards make a meal out of him.

The first mate scuttled off to do his bidding without question. That was good. It meant that the crew didn't think he was responsible for the plague that had descended upon them. Sailors were a superstitious lot, but the captain had never held stock with the ridiculous notions of superstition. But that didn't mean that his crew wouldn't turn on him if more started to die.

He heard the sound of scurrying across the deck. "What the hell was that?" he wondered aloud. Spinning around quickly, he caught sight of movement out of the corner of his eye. It was another rat, a huge one. He chased it across the deck for a few steps, but then stopped due to the pain. After the first couple of steps, the lumps in his groin shot fire through his entire body. He vowed to find a cat when they got to Hamelin. In the meantime, he said a prayer for Old Gert as his body splashed into the river.

The rats watched and listened, the fleas on their backs oblivious to everything but the flesh in front of them and the blood underneath.

Available on amazon!

Printed in Great Britain
by Amazon

16002300R00118